THE PRICE OF THE PHOENIX

"What buys the man without price?" said Omne.

"There is nothing you could offer which would buy me—or your life," Spock said tonelessly.

"Isn't there?" Omne chuckled. The great mirror dissolved into a viewscreen and filled with the image of James Kirk. Unmarked.

"Illusion," Spock said flatly.

"This replica of Kirk is a created object and therefore property. My property, and it is for sale. Would you care to inspect the merchandise?"

The Romulan Commander was suddenly in front of Spock, her hands on his shoulder. "Spock, don't! You must think of him as dead. One step and you are lost."

"Yes," Spock said, to her or to Omne, and put her aside. . . .

THE PRICE OF
THE PHOENIX

Sondra Marshak
&
Myrna Culbreath

BANTAM BOOKS

NEW YORK • TORONTO • LONDON • SYDNEY • AUCKLAND

THE PRICE OF THE PHOENIX
A Bantam Book published under exclusive license
from Paramount Pictures Corporation, the trademark owner
Bantam edition / July 1977
Bantam reissue / February 1993

Star Trek is a Trademark of Paramount Pictures Corporation.
Registered in the United States Patent and Trademark Office.

Joanne Linville's image portraying the Romulan Commander appears on
the cover of this book with the actress's permission.

ISBN 0-553-24635-6

Published simultaneously in the United States and Canada

Bantam Books are published by Bantam Books, a division of Bantam
Doubleday Dell Publishing Group, Inc. Its trademark, consisting of the
words "Bantam Books" and the portrayal of a rooster, is Registered in U.S.
Patent and Trademark Office and in other countries. Marca Registrada.
Bantam Books, 666 Fifth Avenue, New York, New York 10103.

PRINTED IN THE UNITED STATES OF AMERICA

RAD   14   13   12   11   10   9   8   7

To CAROL FRISBIE

Only Carol could have presided over the delivery at the birth of this particular phoenix. Only she, and we, know what kind of prices she paid in day and night intensive care and why, among all the other reasons, our "Bones" is finally getting the last—and first—word.

ACKNOWLEDGMENTS

As always, there is Alan, Sondra's husband. Nothing we do could be done without him. He provides safe harbor, tough advice, practical assistance, vast patience, and—our model for heroes.

As if one person beyond price were not enough, there is also "Mama," Mrs. Anna Tornheim Hassan —without whose endless help we also could not function—our model of a kind of love so rare that it has no name.

And then there's Jerry, five now, who already knows how he can help, and does.

CHAPTER I

Dr. McCoy had one thought in his mind: *Spock must be spared this!* He turned hastily to the next transporter position and took Spock by the arm.

The Vulcan did not even protest as McCoy led him off the platform. McCoy wanted to steer him through the corridors of the *Enterprise*, hustle him to the haven of Sickbay—anything but let the Vulcan stay and see the security men bringing up the stretcher with the bodybag.

But Spock stopped at the transporter console. He planted himself like a rock with that immovable Vulcan strength, and now his peculiar immobility amounted almost to catatonia.

"Energize," Spock said, in a shockingly normal voice.

Scotty stood at the control console himself. He looked blasted, empty, suddenly old. His shoulders struggled to hold themselves at attention, as if they were an honor guard. His hands worked the controls with special care . . . as if it could matter now.

Uhura stood inside the door, neither explaining her presence nor apologizing for the tears which ran quietly down the beautiful dark face.

The transporter shimmered.

The two *Enterprise* security men materialized, took a firmer grip on the anti-grav lifts, and stepped carefully off the platform with the stretcher that bore the body of Captain James T. Kirk.

Spock followed them through the door, his eyes not

moving from the stretcher. McCoy clung to his arm, not sure whether he was giving support or getting it. He could feel the Vulcan's strength. But was it fully sane?

Leonard McCoy knew that he would always remember that quiet procession as nightmare, but it was nothing to the nightmare of going to the planet and collecting the charred body, nothing at all to the nightmare Spock had seen.

Enterprise personnel lined the corridors, stood beside the turbo-lift.

They knew, of course.

Omne had made sure that they knew.

The owner of the hole-in-the-wall planet had announced it bluntly, brutally, sending his special signal through his impenetrable shields which cut off all other communication and piped directly into the ship's intercom. "Captain Kirk is dead. Permission granted for *Enterprise* physician and party to attend."

The crew had not believed it. Their Captain could not die!

Now they read the finality in McCoy's face and in Spock's.

McCoy stopped Spock at the door as the body was carried into the small, sterile autopsy room.

The purpose of the room was only too well known to Spock as a scientist. Standard. All violent or sudden deaths. Dr. McCoy's own strictest rule.

Dr. M'benga was there, raising an inquiring, offering eyebrow at McCoy.

McCoy shook his head. *That* he would do himself. It was the last thing he would do for Jim Kirk.

The Vulcan First Officer looked at him with perfect comprehension. "Thank you, Doctor," Spock said. "He would want that from you."

McCoy found himself without words.

But the Vulcan had spoken—for the first time except for the single order in the transporter room.

McCoy must catch that thread of sanity, draw the Vulcan back somehow to some hold on life.

"Spock—" he began, but the Vulcan was gone again, lapsing into the rigid stare with which he had watched the recovery of Kirk's body from the ashes. The fixed eyes spoke of murder, madness, some terrible release for what could not be released and could not be endured.

McCoy felt certain that Spock's very life was in danger. The Vulcan had survived believing that Kirk was dead once on Vulcan, when Spock thought that he himself had killed his Captain and friend. But the terrible Vulcan emotional control had broken completely in this very room when Spock saw Jim reappear through the door alive. And that was years and many layers of friendship ago. McCoy was not sure that Spock had ever fully believed that Kirk was dead when the Captain had disappeared in the Tholian sector and McCoy and Spock had listened to Jim's recorded last orders together. But Spock had risked the ship on an impossible chance to get Jim back. Still years ago—and what would he risk now, if there were any chance? How would he live with the fact that now there was no chance at all?

The Vulcan repression of emotion was a weakness as much as it was a strength. God knew it had carried the Vulcan through terrible times—sometimes carried them all. But McCoy had always known that it could break down explosively. He had given Spock hell often enough trying to break it down bit by bit before that day would come. This day.

McCoy knew with bleak certainty that this could do it, was probably the only thing which could. He, too, had lost his closest friend. But Spock had lost the only man he had ever permitted really to reach into his self-imposed prison of Vulcan restraint and to touch his naked soul.

McCoy dropped on one knee beside Spock's chair. "Hold on, Spock," he said very softly in the tone of a quotation and almost in another man's voice. "Don't let it break you. Hold on."

The Vulcan shuddered and his eyes reached for the look of comfort Kirk would have offered.

"Thanks, Bones," Spock said very deliberately in the same voice, using the name Kirk would have used.

Then his eyes blazed suddenly with such ferocity as McCoy had only glimpsed. He locked his hands behind his back. "I shall have to 'hold on,' Doctor. Murder has been done, and all hell is about to break loose."

"Murder?" McCoy gasped. "But surely it was an accident? My God, Spock, not even Omne would set that up as a trap. A *suttee*, Sandorian-style? Burn the whole house? The wife? The *baby*? The woman really died, Spock. No trick. Jim just couldn't stand it—not the *baby*. It was an accident."

"Or an exact calculation of the Captain's psychology," Spock said grimly. "It was Omne who staged the delegates' tour of the alien enclaves, lectured us on the Federation's Non-Interference Directive—claiming no Human honored it—marched us in and kept the Captain close, explained to him the custom of immolation, just as the house was fired and the woman dashed in carrying the child. It was Omne's Romulan mercenaries who blocked me when I tried to go after Jim."

He broke off, and McCoy could almost see the flames flare high behind his eyes. McCoy could see behind his own the glowing ashes and Spock still standing locked between burly Romulan renegades, Vulcanoid and as strong as he. Spock still holding a screaming, naked boy baby perhaps six months old. Spock, who couldn't hold a tribble or a cat without petting it, holding the baby and quite oblivious to it. McCoy had taken it from him, parked it almost as obliviously with some woman, tried to question Spock, finally gotten the stock in fragments from witnesses: Spock bowling down Romulans like tenpins, reaching the door, seeing Kirk with the mother clawing at him, holding him. Kirk had pitched the baby to Spock, who caught it just as the Romulans caught him again, and just as the flaming house collapsed with Kirk inside.

McCoy closed his eyes. It didn't help.

But if Spock thought that he had seen murder—maybe his sanity really had snapped. Maybe he had to have somebody to kill. And what would that do to his Vulcan philosophy of peace? Spock's face showed nothing of Vulcan's thousand years of peace. It was the face of his savage heritage, five thousand years deep—or five million.

McCoy's legs were not doing too well. He shifted to the chair behind the desk. Spock was a walking mass of grief, but he was in command of the *Enterprise* now, with power to destroy a planet. There was a war brewing here anyway. This miserable outlaw planet was the intrigue center of the galaxy. And McCoy doubted that Omne's Black Hole was safe now, even behind its impregnable shields.

Spock glanced up and caught McCoy's fixed look. The Vulcan stopped abruptly. He came and settled on a hip on the corner of McCoy's desk—an uncharacteristic pose for him.

"Check my logic, Doctor," he said. "I am not fully—functional."

"Check *your* logic?"

The Vulcan looked at McCoy gravely. "I do not believe that we will need his last orders—this time. Do you?"

"No, Spock. Not this time."

Spock nodded. "Then hear me." He drew back his shoulders until they crackled. "Point one: It is possible that I am being paranoid, but I do not think so. My intuition senses a deeper plot than we knew. Of course, we have confirmed the suspicion that brought us here—that this whole conference of strange delegates, outlaws, renegades, revolutionaries, governments in exile, dissident factions is aimed at breaking up the Federation, perhaps taking many planets into an alliance with the Romulans and enabling them to go to war again. Omne makes no bones about favoring that, nor about his contempt for the Federation. Yet you recall that he greeted us on the viewscreen saying that he was pleased that we had 'accepted his invitation'—implying that he had carefully arranged things so that we would try, as the Captain said, to 'crash the party.' You could not see his first curiously excessive cordiality to the Captain and myself, but when he finally beamed you down to join us on our private tour at the hospital—" Spock cut himself off. "What do you make of him, Doctor?"

"Medical opinion?" McCoy frowned, sourly remembering how he had been left standing foolishly on the transporter while the other two shimmered out and how he had spent a frantic time with Scott while the Engineer determined that the transporter which took them was actually on the planet, working right through the impenetrable shields, and working as if it were the *Enterprise* transporter and responded to its controls. But it was not and did not, and would not take McCoy until he was summoned. Then he saw Omne in the flesh.

"First thought: madman," McCoy said. "Megalomaniac. Delusions of omnipotence. Maybe where he gets the name." He shook his head. "Second thought: not crazy. I know the place is all laid out with the trappings of melodrama and legend, but it has a weird kind of point to it. All the Wild West stuff—" he pointed to the six-shooters on Spock's hip and his own—"but it's 'check your guns at the door'—only equal guns cheerfully provided by the host. Makes for polite society, he says. No law but challenge, and the old equalizers; no back-shooting and the Romulan guards to keep everybody honest. But there are alien enclaves where no guns are allowed, customs strictly their own business. And more than one legend. I saw an ancient Greek section, something that looked Renaissance, the Great Age of Deneb Five."

"Pre-Reform Vulcan," Spock added. "And the time of Surak."

"Looks to me like the old idea of a proprietary community," McCoy said. "Minimum order provided by the host, protection against outside force—the shields. There doesn't seem to be offensive armament on the same scale or a space navy, but the stories have it that a ship cutting up trouble within fifty thousand miles buys the farm. So now it's a free port, a stone's throw from the Romulan neutral zone. Look at us. Three Romulan ships in orbit, and we haven't shot each other up yet. And nearly a hundred other alien ships bringing delegates from three times that many planets."

"Ninety-three. Three-point-two times," the Vulcan corrected automatically.

McCoy nodded. "The man who can do that is taken seriously—and is a serious man. And that hospital— I saw things there I'd give my eyeteeth for—things that don't exist yet in the civilized galaxy. That implies a research capability of a high order. Omne doesn't give himself any title, but he has to be an M.D."

"And a Ph.D. in several scientific fields," Spock added.

"Linguist. Galactic man. Steeped in the languages and literatures of Lord knows how many worlds. Knows colloquial English and slang as well as you do—but he admits it."

Spock raised an eyebrow, but it looked impatient. "Also he speaks Vulcan like a Vulcan. But where does that leave us? A man of power, but to what purpose?"

McCoy remembered the fear which had made him try to keep Jim and Spock from going back for the second meeting, to which he was pointedly not invited. It was almost a physical fear, caused by the mere physical presence of the giant in black, against the costumed and painted backdrop of the private world he had created. The plain black jumpsuit, boots, gloves; the black hair and the unfathomable black eyes; the massive muscle and almost overpowering masculinity. Omne looked Human, but there was something alien under the layers of galactic man. The man was ageless. And there was some aura of brooding, black grief and rage, decades deep.

McCoy shook his head. "Omne scares hell out of me, Spock. He's not crazy, but there's a fixed purpose that's almost as bad. He's—an owner, Spock. He wants to own his world, his way, price no object. Whatever he wants, he'd destroy himself or the galaxy to get it."

Spock nodded. "Poetic, Doctor, but my impression as well."

"Something else, Spock. He's—an alpha male. You know the idea of ranking the dominant males in a primate group alpha, beta, gamma. Jim and I always figured it works for men, too. But this Omne—he's so alpha he'd have a tough time even finding a contest. Maybe *I'm* crazy, and that doesn't have anything to do with it. But I had the feeling he wanted to take us on."

"The—Captain," Spock said with effort.

"And maybe you. Or what you both stand for, the Federation. He has that fixed idea about trampling customs. It seems to be the key issue of the conference. You've even had trouble with it on Vulcan. And that semiofficial Vulcan delegation here—"

"My thought also, Doctor. If a Federation Starship Captain were killed seeming to violate the Prime Directive—"

McCoy drew a deep breath. "But, it didn't have to be murder. A test, a trap, but—" He shook his head. "We'd never be able to prove it. Yes, I think Omne could kill. But *did* he?"

"*That*," Spock said, "is what I have to find out." He stood up abruptly and McCoy went on Red Alert.

"Wait, Spock. *How?*"

Spock paused with the look of barely leashed restraint. "There is more, Doctor. No time to tell you since—the last beam down. The three Romulan ships are, indeed, commanded by our old—friend—the Fleet Commander. She has not forgotten us, nor forgiven.

But she—renewed her offer to me, with variations. Wanting me to defect—and to bring the Captain. I believe that she was trying to warn me of something, as if she knew of it, but could not—or would not—stop it." Spock stopped and the Vulcan jaw set. "Kirk's murder," he said flatly, and there was murder in his eyes.

He turned on his heel and strode through the door.

After a stunned moment McCoy heaved himself up to go after him. But Spock had reached the turbo-lift.

By the time McCoy skated into the transporter room, Scotty was watching a shimmer and turning to say to McCoy, "Would you credit that he left me in command?"

McCoy nodded heavily. "Aye, Mr. Scott, and I wish you joy of it." He slammed his hand on the console. "Damn it to hell, Scotty!"

"Aye," Scott said. "Doctor, is he all right?"

"Are any of us?" McCoy straightened and mounted the transporter. "Give it a try, Scotty." But it was obstinately silent. Spock must have been expected, he thought, and didn't like the thought. He climbed down slowly and collected Scott with a nod. "Come on. I'll prescribe a drink for you. You'll need one. We both will."

CHAPTER II

Spock stepped off the transporter platform where they had first beamed down—in the Wild West section. The Romulan guards in their incongruous black levis and low-slung six-shooters looked at him balefully. One reported into a communicator, but they did not try to stop him as he moved off down Front Street.

It was Dodge City with aircars. It was a dozen legends from a dozen worlds, legends of outlaws and outcasts, hole-in-the-wall gangs and embittered survivors of forgotten wars.

Spock had rated it fascinating and rather pathetic when he first saw it, and had known that it was no less dangerous for all its pathos. Later, seeing Omne, seeing the other legends and the real power, he had seen it as more sinister than pathetic.

He did not see it now; what he saw was a consuming vision of flames, a face, lips which did not scream, but formed the word *Spock!*

Spock raised his left hand to his temple. It was necessary to drive the vision down and back, although he knew that he would see it always. Some such vision in a thousand variations he had seen in nightmares for years.

He reached for the Vulcan technique of discipline and mastery. He was a Vulcan. This was his heritage. There must not be concession to blind emotion, most especially not when the temptation was greatest.

He performed the steps. He concentrated the power and the pride. . .

After a time he took the hand down.

He knew then that he had not expected it to work.

He leveled his shoulders and turned into the conference pavilion. There was still the Human way. He was, after all, half-Human. It would have to do.

The pavilion was a concession to modern technology, providing life-support quarters for a variety of aliens, meeting places for disparate life forms, food and recreation facilities for a number of races. Here in a no-man's-land Omne had created arrangements rivaling those of the official interstellar meeting place at Babel.

Spock found her in the Romulan bar.

There was a drink poured for him. The same orange nectar she had shared with him once on her flagship— once when he lied to her and made her want him, stealing her secret and possibly her heart.

The two square, slender glasses sat in forlorn confrontation. Hers also was untouched.

She stood as he approached and faced him with the manner of the soldier, her eyes understanding that he would not drink with her, that it was an open question whether his first act would not be to kill her.

"You did know," he said.

The soldier's chin lifted. "Not the exact form. Not with certainty. But that there was some danger—yes."

"Specify," Spock said evenly.

She shook her soft hair back from the fine upswept ears. "Such warning as I gave was all that I had to offer—and more than I owed."

He heard her old question—What *are* you that you could do this to me?—and his answer, the only possible answer—First Officer of the *Enterprise*.

If she had wanted her revenge, she had collected it, doubled and redoubled. And if she had wanted to warn him, it was a warning beyond price, and more than she had owed.

"The debt has been paid," he said.

"I could wish that the price had not been so high," she said, as if it were an answer. She shook back the hair again. "You may believe that, if you wish. In any case, the place I offered to make for you is still open. I urge you to take it. There is nothing here for you now. I do not even require your ship. Military hardware is of short-lived value, as we learned. I do not even require a public show. Resign and leave with me this minute." For a moment the woman's eyes looked out of the soldier's face. "I do not claim that I have anything to offer you but refuge. But if you stay, I have reason to believe that you will face danger and grief you will not survive."

Spock shook his head. "There is no refuge. But there is one thing you have to offer which I can accept: that reason."

She shrugged in a gesture of expected defeat. "I cannot tell you. You will have to see it. I wish only to say that Omne is a complex and subtle man. He is not my ally, but certain of our interests have been parallel."

"You believe that Omne murdered Jim Kirk," Spock said, not as a question.

"I perceive that *you* do—and our logic runs on much the same path." She straightened her shoulders. "If it was not murder, it was exceedingly—convenient. Omne's guards will come to escort you to him at any moment. I will go with you—unless you will come with me."

"That would be another decision you would not respect," Spock said gravely.

She sighed. "Mr. Spock, I cannot tell you how tired I am of respecting you."

He raised an eyebrow and turned away.

Six men were approaching. He sheltered the Romulan Commander behind him, careful not to give the appearance of reaching for the Colt revolver Omne had provided him with.

She stepped around him and spoke to the men. "He

will come with us now. Fall in, in close order." Her
hand dropped to her sidearm, slung now in a gunbelt
over her short tunic. She had not been made to surrender her modern weapon. Omne's guards accepted
her authority without question, Spock noted. If she
was not an ally, she was privileged to act like one. Was
she using the privilege for him now? Or merely deliv-
ering him into captivity?

It scarcely mattered. She was taking him where he
wanted to go, and to the one man in the galaxy he
wanted to see.

The one living man.

McCoy bolted into his office and moved blindly toward his chair, only after a long moment registering
the presence of Scotty and a firm hand guiding him.

"You here still?" he grumbled between irritation
and gratitude.

"Again," Scott said. "Checked the bridge. All quiet.
Too quiet. This time I'll prescribe the drink." He was
putting one in McCoy's hand. "You're white to the
eyes."

McCoy nodded, didn't say that he had the right.
Scotty would know where he had been and what he
had been doing in the small, sterile room.

"I suppose there's no mistake," Scotty said. "Androids, doubles, imposters, illusions . . ."

McCoy looked up. God, there was little enough left,
but it was only too real. "Not this time, Scotty. No
mistake."

It had only been the faintest ember of hope, but he
saw it die in the Scot's eyes, as it had died in his own
in the small room he used for autopsies.

CHAPTER III

Spock walked down the length of the great hall toward the figure in black.

He ignored the guards and the Romulan Commander. He could not ignore the memory of Kirk making the same march at his side only this morning: Kirk's little sideways look saying that he distrusted men who made guests make entrances, Kirk's eyes running over the vast tiers of antique books, saying on the other hand that a man who loved books couldn't be all bad, Kirk's eyes noting Spock's interest in a library computer and a sophisticated bank of data-processing equipment, Kirk's eyes incredulous and amused at the bar occupying the back of the hall and outfitted like the Last Chance Saloon, Kirk's eyes and even his body appraising the man in black who rested one foot on the brass rail until he slowly turned to meet them. Kirk knew in his bones and his body how to recognize another man who was born to command, how to estimate the other's dangerousness. Spock knew the signs. Kirk had faced men of power before. Flint, the ageless man who had been Alexander, da Vinci, and all the names of power and mind. Spock's own father, Sarek. Others—the best and the worst of a galaxy. And Kirk's body had said, almost imperceptibly, that Omne was in a class by himself.

Spock shook himself fractionally and faced the man in black again now. He felt that power in Omne himself, but he had long schooled the reaction out of his body, trained himself to stand at Kirk's shoulder and

back him without intruding, content to know that
Kirk relied on that without question.

So many things, great and small, which would not
be again.

Spock looked through the vision of flames to meet
the eyes of the man in black and knew that Omne saw
murder barely leashed and a challenge flung down.
Spock set himself to maintain control sufficient to permit speech to this man.

"My dear Spock," Omne said in the heavy, low
voice, "you are beside yourself."

"It suited me better to be beside him," Spock said.
"You have made that impossible."

"On the contrary," Omne said with a cryptic smile
on his sensual lips, and Spock thought he saw the
Romulan Commander stiffen.

"You have not done it?" she asked Omne hollowly.

"My dear Commander, we speak in riddles, and
Spock speaks of murder."

"Murder," Spock said. "Answer that without riddle
if you wish to have time for riddles."

"But it answers itself, Spock of Vulcan," Omne said.
"Your Captain acted on his own initiative and in
accordance with his character, as you know best of all.
Had I wished to murder him in so spectacular a fashion, I could not have done so without his spectacular
cooperation."

"The moral question does not answer itself," Spock
said. "If you knew that he would do that—"

"No," Omne broke in, "the moral questions never
answer themselves. Suppose that I knew. Suppose that
I knew that he was quite splendid—and that he was
what is destroying the galaxy? Creeping do-goodism.
Maudlin meddlesomeness. Smothering benevolence. I
have established a refuge here from goodness. Deliver
us from virtue—especially the virtuous who prescribe
virtue to others. On that young mother's planet survival is bought at a price. A widow with a young child
cannot survive, would be a burden on her family if she
tried, would watch the child die of slow starvation. But

your Captain did not have to know that. He knew only what he *felt*. He has done it before, is notorious for it. Was. He was a true son of the Federation. Its Prime Directive is written on the wind—and in a trail of blood. Cultures destroyed. Civil wars started. Populations shocked out of existence. Tasmanias—from one end of the galaxy to another—"

"I have heard the view," Spock cut in, knowing how close he had come to speaking it, part of it. But he was Kirk's counterweight on the matter of the noninterference directive, as on other matters. That was both Spock's function and his right. "The argument is irrelevant to the question of murder," he said.

"It is not," Omne answered. "I set him a test. He did not have to fail it—or die in failing. If he had passed, I would have let you both go free. There did not have to be intent to murder."

"You do not say that there *was* not," Spock said.

Omne raised a heavy eyebrow. "You notice that?" He shrugged. "I was willing to give a sporting chance, but I would not expect you to believe that when you hear the answer to the riddle."

"I will hear it now," Spock said with finality.

"You do not answer on the Prime Directive—do not defend him?" Omne said.

"I do not answer murder with words," Spock said, "or defend him to one not fit to have looked on him." He heard the ancient madness in his voice and did not flinch from it.

The Commander touched his arm, but Spock did not look at her. His eyes held Omne's. "You have declared no law here but challenge. State your riddle. Then, if you have the courage of your evils, answer me with your gun—or your body."

Omne laughed. "Behold the peaceable Vulcan!" He threw his head back. "I have found your price, Spock of Vulcan. That is my riddle. What buys the man without price?"

"There is nothing you could offer which would buy me—or your life," Spock said tonelessly.

"Isn't there?" Omne chuckled. His gloved hand brushed across a control stud on the bar. The great mirror behind it dissolved into a viewscreen and filled with the image of—James Kirk. Laid out on a bench. The naked body draped with a thin sheet. The face exposed. Unmarked. Sleeping with that vast innocence which was his alone. Breathing. . .

Spock felt the Commander supporting his arm and straightened as the viewscreen winked out.

"Illusion," he said flatly. His mind saw again the vision of flames. Was there some way that Kirk could have been extracted alive? His mind would neither permit the hope nor confirm it. He had not taken his eyes from the spot, the ashes, the—removal. His hand found his communicator, flipped it before realization struck him.

Omne smiled. "Behold Vulcan memory." Again he touched a control stud. "Allow me to open a channel for you."

"Spock to McCoy," Spock said as if there had been no interruption. There was not even the delay of relay, as if Omne had known Spock's intention and tapped into the intercom. .

"McCoy here." The voice was tired beyond endurance, an answer in itself.

"The—examination," Spock said. "There was no doubt—of—the identity?"

"Doubt?" The voice caught. "No, Spock. No doubt at all."

"Thank you, Doctor. Spock out."

He faced Omne bleakly.

"Quite right, Mr. Spock. The Sherlock Holmes maxim: Eliminate the impossible; whatever remains, however improbable, must be true."

Spock attempted a shrug. "Android," he said. "Alien shape-changer. I could name half a dozen methods—most of them tried—on us." And if it were an android, he caught himself thinking, say—a quasi-biological android like Flint's Rayna, capable of thought, feeling, choice. . .

"Not this one," Omne said. "It is new. I will tell you a story, Mr. Spock—of a man whose planet was peaceably contacted by the Federation. Most peaceably. Most solicitously. Oh, a little bending of the Prime Directive here and there. Nothing major. Earthman's burden. But it led to a civil war—Federation supporters against the old way. The man saw his life-mate killed, along with his sons—some on one side and some on the other. The planet was reduced to rubble and barbarism. The man conceived a hatred of Death. Before he loved again, there would be a way to defeat Death—for the dead to live again. Not his dead, perhaps. But it would be a purpose to keep going on, a kind of ideal." He shrugged. "Ideals are fragile, but purposes endure. The perfect replica, Spock. Identical. Yours, if it is your price."

"Mine?" Spock heard himself saying, then pulled himself up short. "It's not possible," he said. "A ghost, a zombie, a pale imitation. Some obscene sorcery—"

"Science, Mr. Spock." Omne's voice was cool, dispassionate. Only the black eyes glittered with the brightness of fixed purpose. "The final triumph. Immortality. The defeat of Death. Come, we have known for years that we were quite close with the transporter process. But it could only transmit life to life, not death to life. The vital spark was gone. We did not know how to capture it and reinfuse it—"

"It has been tried," Spock said doggedly.

"Not properly." Omne leaned back against the bar, his eyes focusing on some distance. "There are mental emanations, Mr. Spock. As a telepath, you should know. Particularly in a moment of extreme crisis—death, or the ultimate fear of it—they radiate beyond normal limits."

Spock felt the Commander tugging at his arm again and knew that he had swayed. Yes. Through the flames he had seen it, but more: felt it. Felt the "emanations." The astonishment, the unbelief, and finally the belief.

"The nature of such emanations has defeated science for centuries," Omne continued, "but the phenomenon of projection of the whole personality at the moment of death or ultimate terror has been well known. How many fathers, mothers, brothers, mates have reported such a visitation—and from what distances? What is real can be studied. It merely required an approach without preconceptions, and an enduring purpose."

"It would require a whole new theory," Spock said with a heavy effort to focus on the fact.

"Yes," Omne acknowledged. "After which the hardware was relatively easy—merely requiring some years of development. What is real can be recorded. It required only a new type of recorder, and a means of playing the recording back into combination with the basic biological matrix of a transporter scan." He straightened and faced Spock gravely, for a moment without challenge or hostility, merely as if presenting the fruits of his work to a mind capable of understanding. "Every cell, every molecule. And now—every thought, every memory. Identity, Spock, indistinguishable identity. Immortality."

"There would be a difference," Spock whispered, not as a scientist.

"Illogical, Mr. Spock. A difference which makes no difference *is* no difference." Omne moved, dismissing the moment of naked communication. "I do not speak of the philosophical problem, of course. A—replica—is a created object, and therefore property. My property, and it is for sale. Would you care to inspect the merchandise?"

The Commander was suddenly in front of Spock, her hands on his shoulders. "Spock, don't! He is dead. You must think of him as dead. One step and you are lost."

"Yes," Spock said, to her or to Omne, and put her aside.

Omne smiled and bowed Spock toward a door.

CHAPTER IV

Spock snapped to the discipline of logic. There was purpose again now. The door had to lead to the vast underground complex which his tricorder had detected on their first visit—detected but could not penetrate, any more than it could penetrate the outer shields of Omne's whole compound with its huge gates, any more than the starship's sensors or weapons could penetrate the shields of the whole planet.

They moved through the door into corridors of a size to stretch for miles, but turning at odd intervals. There was a turbo-lift, with guards following them in. The lift answered to Omne's voice, giving a number code. Spock's memory took the code in, compared it against numbers he had seen in the short stretches of corridors they had traversed. There was something very odd about the numbering system. He set his senses and the sub-thought level of his mind to calculate acceleration, time, and distance in the turbo-lift. The calculations were accurate, of course.

He did not expect them to do him any good.

A hundred levels—his calculator methodically computed size of the complex and the number of places to hide a captive. He did not bother to reduce it to a number of sufficient accuracy to irritate a Human.

He did not permit himself to hope that he would ever play that game again with a certain Human.

They stepped off the lift near a door.

Omne opened the door and bowed Spock through, unctuously. Spock had expected a laboratory. It took him a moment to recognize the ancient Earth ritual of candles, flowers, and lying in state.

A flame-pot, glowing coals, and a faint scent of incense: the Vulcan equivalent.

Omne was trying to play on his nerves, Spock recognized with cold clarity, and succeeding. But nothing could divert his attention from the slow rise and fall of breath in the broad chest, the flicker under the eyelids in the peaceful, dreaming face.

He moved to stand over the catafalque.

"Sleeping beauty," Omne said. "You may perform the awakening—in the traditional manner, if you like."

Spock shot him a savage look, but could not spare eyes for it for long.

He looked down and was stopped for a moment. He could not use the name. If he used the name he was certainly lost. He unlocked a hand from behind his back and closed long fingers on the bare, warm shoulder.

Surprise. And then a smile played on the still sleeping lips.

Then Spock saw the face relive the moment of astonishment, unbelief, belief. Veins stood out in ridges. The lips formed "Spock!" Stomach muscles knotted and flung the wide shoulders up into arms which caught them. The hazel eyes snapped open.

After a moment they focused. The waking voice whispered, "Spock?" The arms closed on Spock's shoulders.

"Shh—" Spock said and held for a moment, then disentangled and eased the shoulders down, pulled up the fallen sheet. "Rest."

"Rest?" The figure rolled up on an elbow, a sudden wry grin celebrating. But there was puzzlement around the eyes. "In peace—I thought. How—?" The keen eyes searched the room, took in the atmosphere, the two figures in the background, the pointed-eared Romulan guards. "Not a bad version of Hell." The eyes looked back at Spock. "Or—Heaven." A faintly mocking smile. "However, I take it, it is neither."

"Both," Spock said.

"Exactly," Omne cut in. "Allow me to explain. I do not believe that Mr. Spock is able." He moved to Spock's side and looked down, meeting the challenging hazel eyes. "You, sir, presumably remember almost to the moment of death. You would not remember more if you were the real Kirk. You are, however, not Kirk. You are a replica. Kirk revisited."

"In a pig's eye!"

Spock sighed. It was a perfect imitation of McCoy's inflection on a certain similar occasion. This—replica—was trying to tell him that he *was* Kirk. And in fact it was going to be almost impossible not to think of him as Kirk.

"Spock," the familiar voice said. "You haven't answered."

"No," Spock said.

"Then—you believe him? You saw me die?"

"I saw—the house fall," Spock said precisely.

"Damn." The voice was very soft. Spock saw the eyes trace out the progression which would have brought Spock here, the steps, the effort. "I'm sorry, Spock."

Spock nodded without denial, acknowledging the understanding.

"Don't apologize," Omne said, smiling down at the figure. "You are as innocent as any virgin. More than most. A grown man without sin."

"Go to hell." The voice still had that surprising mildness which it gained when the going was toughest. The eyes dismissed Omne and shifted to Spock. "Consider all the alternatives, Spock, but I can tell you—I'm here, Spock. Ask any question. Use the mind link. Whatever. I don't know how he's worked it, but I'm here. Mind, body, everything."

"That is what he claims," Spock said. "Perfection."

"Precisely," Omne said. "My replica would be Kirk and *know* it was Kirk. It would, however, still be my replica."

Spock saw some purpose forming on Omne's face,

but could not read it. "Guards. Commander," Omne called, and as the guards came up: "Position yourselves in back of Mr. Spock and on the other side of this one under the sheet. See that neither makes any sudden moves." He turned to his right toward the foot of the bench where the Commander was now standing. "Commander, there is a question of identity—and—perfection. I believe you knew the late Captain?"

"I have known him to be 'late' before," she said.

Spock winced. He had always suspected that there would come a time when they would rue the day they had faked Kirk's death before her eyes, as they had faked so many other things. There was no likelihood of forgiveness or sympathy.

The figure shifted as the man became aware of his position, trying to arrange it, becoming aware that the sheet was a shimmering thinness—at best, translucent; from certain angles, almost transparent. He bowed his head faintly, putting his best face on the situation. "Commander," he said.

She inclined her head gravely.

No answering name, no title, Spock noted. The unperson treatment. Even as he was doing. Even he.

Omne put his hands on his hips, resting them on the low gunbelt. "Now, my replica. I do not know how well the Commander knew your predecessor, although Captain Kirk was legend for being well known on short acquaintance. However, Commander Spock has certainly shared ship and shore leave for many years. Hardships, injuries, dangers, gym workouts. He must know the Captain very well. Every contour. Every scar. Every injury. There is a half-healed one on your leg. You will therefore stand up and display that identity and perfection."

"Don't be absurd!" the man snapped. His face had been slowly coloring.

"You are property, replica," Omne said. "Move!"

The figure remained carved in stone. "Even if I were a creation, I belong to no man. Spock doubts me. Therefore I am prepared to consider the possibil-

ity that James Kirk died. I know, equally, that I *am*
James Kirk—whatever my origins. And I know that I
am a man, and a mind. A mind cannot be owned, and
a man will not be, must not be. You may be able to
kill me, perhaps even to keep me, but you will never
own me."

"I own you *now!*" Omne's gloved hand blurred with
the speed with which it would reach for a gun, and
stripped the sheet away.

Spock's hand closed on Omne's offending wrist, and
he learned that it was not Human when it did not
break. For a moment he locked with a strength to
match his own, perhaps more than match. Then too
many Romulan arms locked around his shoulders from
behind.

And one vulnerable Human was coming off the
bench with fire in his eyes, undeterred by extraneous
and unpreventable problems.

"No, Jim!" Spock ordered.

And was obeyed.

The Romulan arms locked around Spock were a
kind of needed support. Vulcan eyes locked with Human, and the Human's were very bright and full. It
had always been a part of what they were, Spock
thought, that his Captain would know the moment to
obey.

"This is my Captain," Spock said. "I require no in-
spection,"

"But I require it," Omne answered.

Kirk's eyes never left Spock, acknowledged no other
presence. "And I require it," he said. "Your faith was
what I wanted. It is your certainty I need—and my
own. Use the mind-touch, Spock."

Spock bowed his head, knowing also how to obey.

"By all means, Mr. Spock," Omne agreed. "Feel free
to verify the—fidelity of the reproduction."

The guards eased their holds and Spock straightened.

"It requires privacy," he said.

"It does not, Mr. Spock," Omne said. "I am a stu-

dent of matters Vulcan, as you will learn." He turned
and smiled at the woman. "So much, again, for the
legend that Vulcans cannot lie, my dear. But you
knew that, of course."

"Mr. Spock is fond of unspoken truths," she said.
"This one is that *he* requires privacy, most urgently,
for his friend."

"He is in no position to require it," Omne said. "But
tell me, my dear, what think you of the reproduction?"

"Quite perfect," she said archly. "The original, to
the life."

Spock felt an eyebrow rising and subdued it. She
was not above needling him. There had, of course,
been that long trip to drop her off when she was their
captive—and their guest. He had thought she had
spent it absorbing Human cultures. She would not see
Spock, but. . .

Kirk's face was unreadable, for once.

And Spock prided himself that his own was inscrut-
ably Vulcan.

Then it came home to him what a change there had
been in her attitude—and his own.

The almost metaphysical horror was gone. This Kirk
was real.

The horror returned to Spock with sickening force.
This same Kirk—*his* Kirk—had been killed! This living
body was dead on the *Enterprise.*

And yet it was still impossible not to take this Kirk
as real. Not to take him as a blessing. Could this, indeed, be the defeat of death—even if it were born of
murder?

Spock moved forward and flexed his hands, hasten-
ing and delaying the moment of the mind-touch. What
if he found—imperfection? A less-than-complete copy?
There was still so much. What if he found even—
fraud? That biological android? Some life-form which
could mimic, to the life? Would even that still be—
enough?

And what if he found the real Kirk?
Too much?

For the first time in his life, Spock declared a plague on all philosophical questions.

He took Kirk's face in his hands, not asking this time a permission which had always been granted.

His fingers found the stylized position of the mind-touch and he cleared his own mind of the vision of the flames. He could do it now. He swept mind and body clean of the horror that must not be in the touch.

And he saw the same kind of clearing in Kirk's face, the steadying down to quiet control, the fine courage of the willingness to open.

"How touching," Omne drawled.

Spock felt murder knot in his shoulders again. He did not let it reach his hands.

And then Kirk's hands reached to ease the shoulders and to draw him surprisingly close. "We are alone, Mr. Spock," he said. "Quite alone. Do you understand?"

"Indeed, Captain. Quite alone." And he made it true.

The mind-touch was a lowering of personal barriers. If it did not require privacy, it nonetheless cried for it.

Spock slipped in easily at the level of warmth. He had been here before. It knew how to accept him.

Spock fought to keep the touch narrow, to move quickly up to the cooler level of consciousness. 'Jim?'

'My God, yes! It *is* yes?' Spock heard the soft mind-laughter. 'Hell, yes! Spock?'

'Yes. Indeed, yes!'

Laughter again, rippling like quicksilver. 'Where is my logical Vulcan?'

'Here.'

Sudden catching of breath. 'Even if—it's not—*me*, Spock?'

'It *is* you, all of you, irrespective of anything which has happened. That is my certainty, and your own.'

A shudder, caught and held to stillness. 'Then—it *has* happened?' Steadiness, open steadiness.

Impossible to lie to that.

'I—see no other possibility, but I do not rule one out.'

Deep breath. 'That's it, then.' Spock felt the Human's shock, felt sadness like soft music, anger like flaring fire. His hands felt the fine face steady itself, the head lift. 'It will be hardest for you, Spock. Don't feel—you must force it to be—the same. It's only that I—can't feel—any different.'

' "A difference which makes no difference *is* no difference." '

Spock felt a small, startled ripple in the quicksilver. And a large jolt of gratitude in the stomach muscles. Felt something trying to burst the heart. 'Logician's paradox, Spock? A Vulcanism?'

'Also a Terranism. And—a truth. You have another. "And the gates of Hell shall not prevail against us." '

Perhaps the Human's heart did burst then. The answer was not at the level of words. There *were* words running suddenly along below the level of mind-speech, ancient words, intoning, but the Human thought that he could not say them. Yea, though I walk through the valley of the shadow of death, I will fear no evil . . . for thou art with me . . . There was a bracing of the wide shoulders and a ripple of quicksilver. 'Gates of Hell, Spock. We've broken out of worse places.'

It was for Spock to draw breath now, and he felt as if he had forgotten how for a long time. He drew his consciousness back, reaching for the calculation of necessity which had been proceeding at the sub-thought level. Yes, the logic was clear and must be faced, whatever the cost.

'Jim?' he called, 'James.' It was a name he never used.

Kirk's head lifted. 'Yes?'

'I am going to—mark—you now. It will be—my way back to you, for I think that he will keep you from me.'

'Keep—me?' Cheeks moving to swallow. Jaw firming. 'Mark me, Spock?'

'In the mind. Not to be seen, or counterfeited.'

Puzzled reaching. Sudden jolt. 'You think he could make more—copies?'

'A—possibility.'

'My God!'

Ragged breath. Brow furrowed in thought. Thought racing through consciousness and beyond it, lightning fast and adding to a sum. 'Spock, you have to leave me. He can hold me over your head—forever. He can—kill me before your eyes—and bring me back.'

'Yes. We must assume so.'

'You have to take the ship and go.'

'Not possible.'

'It has to be possible. Otherwise, he can buy you.'

'He can.'

Deep breath. 'No, Spock! I won't have it. Jim Kirk is dead. Go and bury your dead. That's an order, Mr. Spock.'

'A dead man is in a poor position to give orders.'

'Don't chop logic with me, Spock. You said—no difference.'

'None. But your logic is not in the best order, Captain. And you are—temporarily—not in a position to command. Has it escaped you that if he can buy me, he can also sell you—all over the galaxy?'

Stunned silence. The old oaths, suppressed below the level of the mind-voice.

'You see, I cannot leave you here—alive.'

'I see.' Breath. 'Then you have to leave me here dead. Now.'

'No.'

'Spock—'

'You are not to think of yourself as expendable. Would I kill Jim Kirk? You are he, no less. No difference. You have been a captive before.'

'I will not be—your price.'

'You have been that before, too.'

Spock felt the stunned silence in the other's body. Then the Human sighed deeply. 'All right, Spock.'

Spock found himself wanting to retreat behind the

wall of Vulcan restraint, but he did not. 'You are exceptionally obedient for once, Captain. I approve.'

The ripple of quicksilver responded to the Vulcan's effort at lightness, as he had intended. 'Yes, Captain Spock, sir.'

'That is better. We may not have much time. You will kindly endeavor to apply logic to the problem—'

'Spock,' the quick mind cut in, sobering. 'You said—mark me. How? Wouldn't that duplicate, too?'

'No. I would attempt—a special kind of mind-link. It would lead me to you. This underground is a labyrinth, designed as such. You can be moved, hidden in the maze. That link is our only chance. If you—died, I would feel it—go. If he—copied you, I would feel—something. A difference.'

'What are you waiting for?'

'It requires your permission.'

'Well?'

'With—knowledge. There is a danger. I am primarily a touch-telepath. This link would have to be deep, directional, binding at a distance. It has never been attempted for such purpose. I would—take care. But you would still find the depth disturbing.'

There was a tap on Spock's shoulder.

Kirk felt the tap, too. 'Do it, Spock. Now!'

Spock shifted his grip on Kirk's face. There was no precedent for this, no words which could be used. Only the necessity of reaching deep, quickly, deeper than ever, a swift agony of barriers to be broken, reaching through to layers and levels and hidden places which wanted and did not want to be touched, gathering up gossamer strands of the link into a slender, indissoluble thread.

The Human gasped and sagged against the Vulcan. A moment of rebellion, no, not to be so close, so open, no. The rebellion put down. Necessity. Then, finally, being able to bear it, to reach for it, to reach back. Yes.

A gloved hand ripped Kirk's hand off Spock's shoulder.

Words, after all. Quickly now. 'Gates of Hell, James.'

Breath. Weak ripple of quicksilver. Solemn sunlight glinting off silver waves. 'Shall not prevail . . . Worse places, Spock.'

Omne was pulling Spock away, flinging Kirk toward the bench. The Human turned and caught himself against it, sagging, fighting now also against the pain of the sudden tearing out of the upper levels of the link.

Spock set his teeth and fought also—with that, with Omne, with himself not to try to kill Omne now. There would be no chance against all of the guards. Worse, there could be no way to keep the Human out of it—against the Vulcanoid muscles and bones of the Romulan guards. And against—this Omne. Of Vulcanoid strength, at least, although he looked Human. But there was nothing Human in the giant's weight, strength, speed—and the size—outreaching Spock in every dimension. Omne. What *was* he?

Spock strained against the giant, carefully, gauging strength against the time when it would be in earnest, leashing the blind desire to kill, until Romulan guards caught and pinned him, and he stood quiet.

Kirk was regaining his composure, pulling himself up.

Omne smoothed down his jumpsuit with an unruffled look and smiled savagely. He waved the guards off Spock and turned to him challengingly, hooking a thumb at Kirk.

"Well?" the big man demanded.

Spock made a pose of having difficulty remembering the question. In fact, it was not entirely a pose. And there was the question of the answer. One must take exactly the right line with Omne. "Oh," Spock said finally, "the—fidelity of the reproduction is excellent." He took a breath. "May I ask the price?"

Omne grinned with a certain appreciation. "The usual," he said. "Your soul. Your honor. Your home. Your flag."

"Done," Spock said. "Wrap him up and I'll take him with me."

Omne rumbled. He roared. He threw back his head and wiped his eyes. "I do like your style, Mr. Spock!"

"Spock!" the Romulan Commander said.

"Never mind, my dear. I'm sure Mr. Spock understands that it isn't quite that easy." Omne looked at Kirk. "We shall have him around for a time yet. We— deliver, Mr. Spock. See that you do the same."

Spock bowed faintly.

Kirk straightened and turned, putting on his best Kirkian manner like a suit of armor. "See that you do nothing of the sort, Mr. Spock. That's an order."

"I shall give it due consideration, Captain."

"Mr. Spock," Omne said, "I will buy you a drink while we work out the details."

"The details will suffice without the drink," Spock said mildly.

Omne looked at him rather grimly, but finally decided to grin. "Very well, Mr. Spock, we won't haggle. Everybody out! Captain, you will find somewhat more comfortable quarters through that door, but no exit. My compliments on your fidelity. And your First Officer."

"My compliments—to him," Kirk said.

They left him still standing naked amid candles and flowers. But Spock felt a slender bond stretching between them like a strand of steel and gold.

CHAPTER V

Omne started to seat the Commander at the green baize-covered poker table near the bar. She froze him out quietly with her soldier's manner and sat down as though she were dealing herself into the game.

Spock gave her a small salute with an eyebrow, suspecting that she did not like Omne's "my dear" approach any more than she had liked the faint trace of it in Kirk's manner years ago.

There might be some use in that, if Spock could determine what game she was playing.

Spock sat down, watching Omne turn a chair to straddle it and reach out to pour a drink, pass one to the Romulan Commander, riffle a stack of chips which were ancient American double-eagles. Spock was becoming insufferably tired of the man, his macho mannerisms, his toys. That was danger, Spock recognized. The man used all of that, for that very purpose.

But Spock had learned poker from Jim Kirk. He betrayed no impatience, made Omne speak first.

"I see," Omne said. "Very well, Mr. Spock, we understand that you have not, after all, conceded so easily. We have merely established the value of the stakes, have we not? A no-limit game."

"No limit," Spock said. "State your details."

"Quite simple. Have you wondered why this was aimed at you?"

"The thought has occurred."

"A convergence, Mr. Spock. On you. As Vulcan

goes, so goes the galaxy. As you go, so goes Vulcan. I have become aware of the importance of your family there and the effort of your father and yourself to keep Vulcan from breaking with the Federation over the matter of Human interference with alien customs."

Spock shrugged. "That effort does not depend upon me. My father—and Vulcan—will not be impressed by anything I do under duress."

"Ah, but you will not appear to be under duress. Therefore, the necessity of giving you a plausible reason to appear to recognize the error of the Federation—and of your friend—in his very death. More in sorrow than in anger, you will denounce him—and the galaxy rallies to the cause of the great, brooding figure from Vulcan. That is your script."

Spock felt his jaw hardening and a gulf opening in front of him. The man had an understanding of what would work. And an unlimited evil. Poker, Spock told himself. "There is a flaw in your theory," he said. "By that script you could not intend to let Kirk leave with me alive. Therefore I would not do it."

"Second point of convergence, Spock," Omne said, looking again at the Commander. "The Commander—wants you." He shrugged and spoke to her. "That's your business, my dear. But as you go, so goes the Romulan Empire. My script for Spock will benefit you, too, by bringing my alliance to life, and you will commit the Empire to defend it. That combination will free you of the trap of the Romulan Neutral Zone and make you strong enough to challenge the Federation. You get your brooding Vulcan—and the bonus of a slightly disguised friend whom you can hide in the vastness of the Empire."

"The flaw in that theory," she answered smoothly, "is that you need the Empire far worse than I need you."

"The flaw in *that*," Omne said, "is that *I* have the price of the priceless Spock."

She shrugged. "Mr. Spock is not my price, or he could have bought me long ago. I am the buyer."

Omne spread his hands. "Perhaps he was not for sale at your price."

Her shoulders stiffened, but she smiled at Omne. "I will make you a counteroffer: immediate support of the Empire, which should breathe life into your alliance without benefit of the Spock script. And all I want is—a certain reproduction. The print and the negative. The matrix."

Omne laughed. "All? That would give you Mr. Spock's price. And—the priceless. That would very likely give you enough information to figure out the process, and the process could buy the galaxy."

The Commander nodded. "That thought has occurred."

"Very astute, my dear." Omne leaned back, gripping the back of the chair, flexing the muscled arms which the thin black silk sleeves of the jumpsuit displayed to advantage. "Perhaps more than I had thought. What would you like to be? Empress of the Empire and Commander in Chief? With Spock as Prince Consort and Kirk as an attendant lord? You could do it with my process. There is no Empire, no Federation, no planet, no starship, which does not have a key man with a wife, a child, a friend. Of course, I have no intention of releasing the process. However, I might use it for you on occasion. I fear you are a trifle squeamish, my dear."

"If I wish murder done," she said, "I will do it myself. You understand that while you have the process, you cannot be allowed to live?"

Omne laughed. "The lady raises the bet." He shook his head. "No, my dear. You don't have the chips or the cards for this game. I cannot be threatened. The man without love gives no hostages to fortune. While my shields hold, your three ships are as powerless as Spock's *Enterprise*. If I cannot deal with you, I can deal with the Empire—eventually. And if not, I do not truly need the Empire. It would merely be a convenience at the moment. The Federation is the great, unbalanced power to which I must pose a counter-weight—for the freedom of the galaxy."

"Do not pose as a champion of freedom," Spock said flatly, gesturing toward the screen, the underground, Kirk. "You buy and sell—slavery."

Omne shrugged. "There is the political, Spock, and the personal. You are apt to believe, as the day reveals its surprises, that my purpose is merely personal, merely malevolent. I caution you against that. No man of importance is merely a villain, and none can act without some belief in the worth of his cause." He smiled. "Even an outlaw is entitled to a hell-busted ideal or two."

"A murderer is not," Spock said, losing the sense of the playing of poker. Jim had taught him to play, and Jim was—dead.

Omne shrugged. "I am at war, Spock. I have made no separate peace. The galaxy is being taken over by super-empires, including yours—especially yours, with its noble pretensions and even noble aspirations. Nothing is more dangerous than nobility. Your Kirk has been the noblest and deadliest peacemaker in the galaxy. If he were allowed to go on, there would soon be one wall-to-wall empire, sickeningly sweet and subtly oppressive. In conflict there is room for enclaves of freedom."

"Where you can keep a slave?" Spock said implacably.

Omne spread his hands. "There is also the personal, the elemental. Domination is the natural instinct of man, Spock, born of the jungle. We are all wolves here."

"One of us is," Spock said, looking at Omne. He let the fire flare in his own eyes. "Two."

Omne smiled a curious smile—rather like the smile of a wolf. "Three," he said, "even the she-wolf."

"You have no political purpose," Spock said, "only the malevolence of the wolf."

"There you are wrong, Spock," Omne said soberly.

"However, it is also true that I have a personal stake in seeing your own performance."

"What stake?" Spock said.

Omne laughed. "When I buy the man without price, I wish to see whether you have the honor to stay bought, Vulcan."

Spock shrugged. "What else?"

Omne looked at him very solemnly. "Call it—enduring purpose, Mr. Spock. The lie you speak will be a truth a certain man learned decades ago when he watched love die." The black eyes looked through Spock into some distance, then snapped back with a glint as cold as space. "Or say that I cannot stand to see a man who dares to love even in the face of death—even when he gives such a hostage to fortune."

Omne's gloved hands suddenly shoved the stacks of golden chips into a heap in the center of the table and clenched into fists in the heap. "The best either of you can do is call. Spock! Your word on your script. Commander: the alliance and refuge for two fugitives. If Mr. Spock's performance lacks luster, I will give you a slightly used copy—when I have finished with it."

Spock knew that he kept the muscles along his jaw from jumping. "I will not accept damaged merchandise," he said, "and I advise you not to believe that *I* cannot threaten you."

Omne inclined his head. "If there is a man alive who could, Mr. Spock, you are the man. But I hold the high card. Do you call?"

"I call," Spock said.

"Commander?"

"I am in," she said.

Omne dismounted from the chair and stood up, took his untouched liquor glass, and raised it in salute as the Commander and Spock stood up. "Spock, the delegates meet in two hours to discuss the implications of the shocking event of this morning. It should give you time to compose a suitably convincing script along the lines sketched. It must convince *me*. I need hardly say that the hostage answers for your behavior with his person. Commander, a word with you as my new ally—and I believe that we should see to the comfort of the merchandise." He lifted the glass. "To business—the buying and the selling." He drained the liquor in one smooth sweep, but the black eyes remained cold and unblinking. "Guards, escort Mr. Spock out."

CHAPTER VI

The Commander had watched the Vulcan out, and known how close he had come to making his stand there across the gold-heaped table—with the lone six-shooter against Omne and a dozen guards.

And she knew that part of what stopped him was his doubt of her.

If he could have counted on her even to be neutral. . . But she could not explain her position in front of Omne.

And it would not have helped, neither the explanation nor the position.

There was not even a legend that Romulans could not lie.

It was necessary for Omne to believe Spock was not her price, but she suspected that it was Spock who had believed her. He had half-believed her about Kirk. "The original—to the life."

She caught herself smiling. The Vulcan deserved that. And the Human, too. He would have been in there pitching if he had not regarded her as staked out as private property by Spock.

They would learn something about property. Perhaps too much.

She did not look at the burial bier as Omne ushered her silently through the candled room. The flowers meant nothing to her.

At the inner door she raised her hand to tap.

Omne picked the hand out of the air and drew it

38

down to her side, held it against her lunge for her side-arm. She had killed men for less.

He saw it in her eyes and laughed silently.

She controlled herself. His strength was more than equal to holding her, certainly, unless she used advanced all-in-combat techniques.

It was not yet a time for war.

He touched the opening stud and led her in by the hand, unannounced.

Kirk sat up suddenly on the bed, startled, indignant, embarrassed now as he had had the will not to be when he was naked. He wore a short robe which was some kind of cross between an all-in-combat jacket and a hospital gown, and she suspected that he wore it backwards. The edges did not quite meet across chest and hips, and the string ties were of no assistance. Moreover, it was done in some fabric which looked like thin white velvet and clung like a live animal. There was some kind of brief in the same fabric which was supported by a low band around his hips, and provided, possibly, moral support.

He swung soft white boots to the floor and stood up. The edges of the robe fell a trifle further apart and soft folds of fabric shifted, but he had regained the control not to tug at anything. He brought his hands together in the Human military posture of parade-rest, and his manner announced again that he was clothed in dignity.

"Where I come from," he said, "and in the civilized world, the custom is to ask permission to enter."

"One does not ask permission of property," Omne said.

"We have had that argument before."

Omne smiled. "You lost."

"Force is not an answer to argument."

"It is the last answer."

Kirk shook his head, not deigning to answer.

The original, she thought, to the life. She found that she was holding her breath. Yes, she could understand well enough why he was the Vulcan's price.

Omne turned to her as if reading the thought. "And what price would you pay for this one, my dear—if I were not practically throwing him into the bargain?"

"Irrelevant, since you are."

"Not quite," he said. "If Spock convinces me—and the delegates—presumably you will have this one, too, but as a refugee, not property. And if he does not—I am singularly hard to convince—then you would have this one as property, presumably with Spock trying to buy him. But in either case, there could be some question of the condition of the merchandise. For example, his appearance would have to be altered. Romulan ears and eyebrows you presumably would not mind. I believe you have seen them on him before. But there could be other changes. And other damages."

"I would not take Spock's threat lightly, if I were you," she said, seeing Kirk's face working at remaining set, the fine, slanting muscle in the jaw betraying him fractionally.

Omne saw it too, but kept an eye on her. He shrugged. "The planet is impregnable. This compound is a fortress. The underground is a maze, with chambers which even I have not seen for twenty years."

"Spock has a life span of perhaps two hundred years left to breach the impregnable," she said. "He would use all of it."

"He has perhaps two hours to storm the fortress and thread the maze. Two hours which we could better employ." Omne's eyes raked over Kirk slowly, and his massive arm twisted hers and drew her against his side. She could feel the heat of his body through his black silk and her tunic. "There is really no need to wait. Spock will be glad enough to accept damaged goods. If it comes to that, he will have no choice. Moreover, this one would never tell. Your old enemy, Commander, who made a fool of you in front of the Empire and the galaxy! Wouldn't you like to see the Starship Captain beg?"

"What I like is that he would not beg."

She saw Kirk's eyebrows rise in astonishment.

Omne jerked her to face him. "I think he would, ally. Would you care to make a small wager?"

"I will wager that I can kill you where you stand unless you unhand me and leave this room."

Omne chuckled. "Lady, I admire your notion of odds," he drawled. "You are nearly as interesting as the priceless price. But what's your game? Don't you know that you'll never have the Vulcan while this one lives?"

"I'll never have him if this one dies. And you will never have ally or Empire if you harm him. Your bet was called, Omne. If you have no honor, I have. Spock has his two hours and his chance to pay his price. He'll get what he pays for—undamaged—or one of us will die in this room."

Omne twisted her arm up behind her back. She set her teeth and saw Kirk gather himself. She needed the one break against an opponent of Omne's strength and size. It was comforting to realize how certain she was of getting it. If she could have this game Human willingly, at her back or at her side, and the Vulcan at her right hand, the universe could not stand against them.

But that was a dream.

Omne laughed, whirled her, and tossed her into Kirk's arms. The black glove blurred and the ancient Colt was in his hand, looking like the deadly weapon it was. "I can't tell you how you terrify me, my dear," he grinned. "Perhaps I should say, my dears. However, your point is well taken, Commander. I am not a man of honor. Our alliance does not depend upon my honor, since you know my motives and my power. It does depend upon yours, and I shall hold you to it. You also called the bet. I'll permit you to keep this one safe for your Spock while we determine whether your Spock is a man of honor where this one is concerned. I have never allowed my satisfaction to depend upon a particular piece of property."

He bowed, and there was some expression in his eyes which she wished she had not seen.

"And with that thought, I will leave you," Omne said, and backed through the door.

Her hand fell to her sidearm, but she abandoned the impulse. Omne was quick and cautious and on his own territory. He might only wish to draw her out away from Kirk.

Kirk turned her slowly in his arms, and she did not resist. "Thank you," he said simply. And after a moment, "Somehow I don't think Spock would mind if I thanked you properly."

She pulled his head down into the kiss, suddenly grateful that there was neither Romulan nor Vulcan need for ritual gesture and slow propriety. She lived between the stars and so did this one. So, really, did the Vulcan, but there was much he could learn about the joys of abandoning custom. She would teach him, but there might not be much that she could teach this one.

He was not used to the strength which had pulled his head down, but he had resisted it for only a heartbeat, then relaxed and trusted himself into it, concentrating a certain power of his own on taking her breath away.

On that contest, they were about even, she thought. But presently he lifted his head and she let him, let him gather her head to draw her face against his temple and cheek. He held her for a long moment. "I think he would mind more," he said softly into her ear and brushed it with his lips, then slowly drew back from her, still holding her at a little distance.

"You are welcome," she said with a straight face, and saw his eyes light with a glint of mischief.

"You'd have to take that up with Spock first," he said with a little smile which was nevertheless serious.

"I intend to."

He raised an almost Spockian eyebrow, undeterred by the fact that the other one got into the act. "A—custom of your people?"

"No. A custom of my own. I call it 'thinking beyond the phalanx.' Phalanx is not the word. But there are certain military problems which cannot be solved inside the standard military formations." She smiled, also seriously. "Other problems, too. And other—formations."

He nodded. "I know the concept. Get out of the box. Change the name of the game." He shook his head thoughtfully. "You might find that Spock and I are further outside of the phalanx than you know. In fact, I seem to be out of all boxes whatsoever." He looked at the door. "Except this one." He took her shoulders in his hands. "Commander, I can't see the future, and I can't wipe out the past—even if I never lived in it. I know you are supposed to be the enemy, and have cause to be mine. But you just acted as a friend, to Spock and to me." He slipped his hands down to hers and lifted them. "Friends? And—allies? Where honor permits and purposes do not cross?"

She took his hands. "That will do for a beginning." She let her eyes laugh and disengaged her hands, guided his right one into a fist until their right wrists crossed in the Romulan warrior gesture, which could mean in its degrees from first comradeship to the blood-bond of brothers of the sword. It was she, and a few like her, who had made it include sisters.

He looked a little startled, but seemed to regard it as self-explanatory, and returned the pressure gravely and at attention.

She nodded and stepped back. "Now," she said, glancing over her shoulder at the door, "about this box . . ."

"The lock is efficient," he said in the tone of a briefing. "No exit. Your weapon might do for the lock. Omne is another question." He took a deep breath. "I didn't like the look of him."

"No."

"Going to take hell out on somebody." A thought hit him as if it had struck him in the stomach. "Damn! 'One particular piece of property.' Spock thinks there could be other—copies."

She turned to the door, tried it, aimed the beam of

her sidearm. The metal was tough. Only a pinpoint beam would even touch it. "This will take too long," she said, continuing the cutting. "I am the one who should have thought of it. I got Omne to slip a bit on a confirmation. He as good as admitted that a—matrix—can be used to make more copies."

He stood at her shoulder and was silent. After a moment, he said quietly, "In front of Spock?"

"Everything was in front of Spock," she said. "Omne practically drew him a picture, then had him marched out. He'll never get back through those gates."

"The gates of Hell," he said, and one fist impacted into the other.

Then she thought that the sound had been repeated. No. The sharp snap of a remote switch tripping. She cut off the beam and turned to her right to find him watching a large wall mirror dissolve into a viewscreen . . .

They saw the back of another man watching another viewscreen, and his was split-screened into fourths. She recognized the main hall, the candled room, this room . . .

And she recognized the man's back. Unmistakably, it was Kirk. Some Kirk. There was shimmer dissolve to another camera angle showing that Kirk's face. Then came a meeting as if of both Kirks' eyes as the two back-figured from the angles and spotted the hidden cameras.

She located the one in this room herself. There was a tiny prism-lens in the jeweled goldwork of the mirror-screen frame.

But she could hardly take her eyes from the other Kirk, and she found her hands on this one's shoulders.

The two looked at each other.

The other wore a Star Fleet uniform, the tough gold fabric of his command shirt more than faintly scorched. That would be easy enough to fake, she thought. But the hands and face looked slightly seared, too, as by sunburn, and the left hand had a darker streak of red bordering a blister. That was possible to fake too, she supposed.

But the Kirk under her hands knew. And she felt the shoulders sag—and straighten. "Have you been watching from the beginning?" he asked the other.

The other's eyes leveled. She hoped never to see such a look in a man's eyes again, and knew that she would have given all she owned for the privilege of seeing it this once: support, comfort, a searing rage devoid of pity, the respect of a straight answer. "I never lost consciousness," Kirk said.

Her Kirk nodded. She alone could feel what it cost in his shoulder muscles. "How?" he asked.

"He used some new variation of the transporter. It was silent. Half a wall fell in front of me and most of the roof on top of me and a body beside me. My guess would be that it was an incomplete duplicate. But I was already on my way."

"Spock couldn't have seen . . ."

"The wall that fell between us didn't fall by chance. Nor the body—probably stashed in the rafters. I got—just a glimpse."

"The perfect murder," her Kirk said slowly. "And—nobody died."

Kirk nodded. "Except— You wouldn't know about the woman."

Her Kirk tensed. Impossible not to believe that Kirk, but— "How would *you*?"

Kirk wiped it away with a gesture of his hand. "He had viewscreens set up here from the moment I picked myself up off the platform. I saw the collapsed house. Spock. Bones. Bodies. You surrounded by equipment, then Omne moving you . . ."

"My God." She knew that the original Kirk now saw much the same searing look in this one's eyes. "Omne wanted you to see that. For that there is no excuse even in madness. For that, or for what he did to Spock."

Kirk nodded. "Nor for what he has done to you."

Her Kirk caught his lip between his teeth, his brows

drawing together. "We will think about what he has done to me if we both live. Right now—is there any way out for you? Any weapon?"

Kirk shook his head, smiled grimly. "The gun he gave me was useless." The big room he was in was bare except for a few heavy pieces of furniture, too solid to take apart.

Her Kirk turned to her. "Get back to work on that door." She obeyed, but couldn't help glancing at them from the corner of her eye. "You understood what Omne said here," her Kirk continued. "He must have switched the screens on because he wants us to see it happen to you."

"I know," Kirk said quietly. "I've had more time to think about it."

"Don't take any chances. Do whatever you have to do. Kill him."

Kirk grinned soberly. "That doesn't look so easy from here."

"Do you have any idea of your location?"

"I got a guard to open a door. The number was U-27-E-14."

Her Kirk laughed. "That's one break. Made, not born. That's as good as a road map. Hold on."

Kirk grinned. "We'll play a couple of 'macho' games. Domination. Alpha-male stuff. Lords of the jungle. Baboons and breast-beating. Will the Starship Captain bow his stiff neck? That ought to hold him for a while. I do recommend, in all logic, that you hurry." There was a sound off to his right, a door opening, and he turned. Turned back for an instant. "Thank you, Commander. Friends?" But he had to turn to face Omne as the big man moved into the field of view.

"Captain," she warned quickly. "He is not Human. The strength is Vulcanoid. Think of Spock—at nearly twice his weight."

CHAPTER VII

Kirk grinned quick, rueful thanks at the Commander and turned back to face Omne.

He felt his mouth go dry and the knot in his stomach tighten, and knew that he was moving on the balls of his feet, circling, finding clear space, not having to think about the body signals which made it a giving of ground that was not a retreat, but thinking about them anyway. Alpha-male stuff, he had said. He was pretty good at that. Usually he was content to let it operate mostly at the level of instinct. This would take more than that. It was tough as hell when that kind of dominance had to cross the gulf between species with different strengths. You wouldn't think it would operate at all, but it did.

Omne did not have to have Vulcan strength to scare him; there was a power in the man which was only too apparent, whatever world he came from, and an indomitable fighting will which would see the body it drove broken apart before it would yield.

That was a quality of mind, not of muscle.

Omne recognized it in him as well as he in Omne. Somewhere each of them had learned to use it, not only on the level of instinct. Omne could play games with it, and play for keeps.

But also Omne had Vulcan muscle to back it up.

And Kirk had learned too well what that could mean.

"So," he said with the deceptive mildness which let

the deception show through, "that makes it interest-ing."

"Not all strong men in the galaxy are Vulcan, Cap-tain." The bow of a black eyebrow made it an acknowl-edgement.

Kirk inclined his head. "No. Only some of the best."

"And the best plays beta to your alpha." Omne smiled. "I will say it for you, Captain. That makes you good, very good. You sail the stars and take on all comers. Somehow that is even more attractive in one so vulnerable."

Damn, that was a dangerous package. Kirk laughed. "By the same token, it makes me not so vulnerable. I've been up against two, three, five times my strength, maybe more. Vulcans, mutants, androids. It is not a question of muscle."

Omne shook his head, his smile indulgent. "Other things being equal, it *is*, Captain." He moved closer to Kirk, the panther stride emphasizing quickness, the towering width underlining difference.

Kirk stood his ground, looking up without apology to meet the black eyes, his muscles set for a kick and roll if this was to be it.

Omne laughed and stopped, towering over him. "But you would meet few to equal you in other things, Captain. Mind, will, decision. The all-out streak which yields to no man. Death before dishonor. The stiff neck and the straight spine. Backbone. Bluff. The al-pha male is half bluff and all guts." He gestured to-ward the screen; he must have been monitoring. "I, too, am a student of the jungle, Captain."

"Then let's knock this off," Kirk said, shifting with a posture of dismissal. "Who is bluffing whom? At what game? There are more serious matters between us."

Omne shook his head, not responding to the change of posture. "This *is* the serious matter, Captain. Games are always the serious matter. The game of gunsmoke on Front Street. The game of galactic confrontation."

"You are playing games with lives."

"Certainly. Those are always the stakes."

"Murder is not a game to me," Kirk said, "and I am not playing."

"But you are," Omne said, gesturing over his shoulder toward the screen. "You—both of you—just declared intent to murder me—in violation of every law you own, by the way. And I have not even done murder."

Kirk brushed it aside with a hand. "Self-defense. No cop-outs, Omne. You have. And you have done worse. You've caused all the grief of murder. I don't know how to name the other grief. But the woman died."

"Suicide," Omne said. "It was her right and her custom. I did not arrange that, merely used it. I have created a haven here for custom and free choice, even the wrong choice. The first principle of freedom is the right to go to hell in your own handbasket."

Kirk shook his head. "Provided that it is your own hell, your own handbasket—and you don't take passengers who have no choice. Such as a baby."

Omne spread his hands. "It's not possible to have it both ways, Captain. Custom is custom, or it is not. Noninterference is noninterference, or it is not. Anything else is moral judgment on the basis of feeling—and the self-indulgence of imposing your gut reaction on the universe."

Kirk straightened gravely and stood quiet. "No," he said solemnly. "It *can* be—which is the reason for having a Prime Directive. But there is a logic to moral judgments, and there are judgments which have to be made. That is the reason for having men who will make them on the tough ones. Right or wrong, but make them and stand responsible. There is no sanctity to custom. The many can be as wrong as the one, and antiquity as wrong as tomorrow. The sanctity is in life—and in the freedom needed to preserve and enjoy it. Custom is the frozen form of men's choices, not to be shattered lightly, but it does not abolish the need to choose."

Omne was looking at him thoughtfully, one eyebrow rising. "So—you *are* the true antitheses," he said.

"No mere thoughtless bundle of reactions, and no apologist, but the true son of moral certainty." He nodded as if pleased. "It was what I had wanted to learn."

"To what purpose?" Kirk said. "You are no champion of justice. That is a pose. Your real character stands revealed today: killer, kidnapper, plotter, buyer and seller of bodies and souls."

Omne shrugged.

Kirk stood silent for a moment, some part of him impressed. Omne's black eyes were opaque pools of a pain not to be sounded.

The man who owned those eyes was a giant. And a monster.

"No," Kirk said steadily. "I do not grant you the name of a real man.

The giant's black-gloved hand impacted flatly against Kirk's jaw and he went down. It had been only a slap—and it was all but a knockout blow, all but broke his neck.

"Elemental needs," Omne said, standing over him. "Spock can have the copy. I will keep the original."

Kirk rolled away and came, too slowly, to his feet, fighting down blackness and fear. It was not possible to stand against that strength for long.

"Go to hell," he said softly.

Omne nodded. "You will make a delightful handbasket, my proud Captain."

"You don't own the merchandise." Kirk launched a feint and leap which would carry him past the big man's holstered gun. He had nothing to prove about muscle. Take no chances. Kill.

Omne picked him out of the air.

Steel arms crushed him against the corded and molten steel of the big body, his chest against the spring-steel barrel chest, the other's gloved hands digging into his back and thigh. His left arm was pinned too far from the gun at Omne's right, but he chopped with the other hand, reached with the left for the gun.

Omne bent him back with a wrench that threatened his spine. The black eyes looked down into his and a hand moved to twist his left arm up behind his back. The fingers digging into the top of his thigh supported his whole weight, and felt as if they would part muscle, snap bone.

"Learn about muscle, vulnerable one," Omne whispered. He pulled Kirk back against his chest, twisted the arm up into a slow agony, clamped an arm around ribs which strained in protest.

Kirk felt the blackness rising again and a scream clawing at his throat, choking him with the effort to hold it back. God, the man was like Spock unleashed. Spock . . . If he were here . . . there would be Vulcan steel fingers clamping into the massive black shoulder. . .

Suddenly Kirk realized that his chin was above that shoulder, not far from Spock's neck pinch spot—from a good spot for any chop.

He brought his chin down with all his strength and his knee up between the muscled legs.

The knee didn't connect fully, but the chin did, and it was enough. He jackknifed out and away as the hold loosened and the big man swayed, half-doubling and shaking the massive head.

Kirk landed off balance, out on his feet, but tried to come back in to follow the advantage. There would be no second chance. But the bone-bruised thigh gave suddenly under his weight and he fell. He turned the fall into a scissors chop of his legs which cut Omne's feet from under him. The giant fell hard, but caught himself like a cat, rolling up to a crouch.

Kirk came up on one knee and a hand, dazed. Watching warily and trying to rub feeling back into the nearly paralyzed thigh.

The big man straightened only too easily, not really much hurt, and started toward Kirk.

Kirk waited, deciding that he regretted only that the knee had not done its full work.

He doubted that he could stand, but he braced to move. He'd get in a shoulder block, try to bring the giant down.

But Omne stopped. "That, too, is what I wanted to learn."

"To what purpose?" Kirk asked. "To prove the obvious? That big is big?"

Omne smiled and shook his head. "To prove that you will not quit, even against *me*."

Kirk straightened onto both knees and shrugged fractionally. "Who are you that I should quit against you?"

"The man who will make you quit." Omne moved closer, towering.

Kirk looked up and sat back onto his heels. "I am everything which you are not."

"No, Captain. You are everything I might have been."

"And for that, you want to destroy me?"

"No, Captain. I want to own you, to own—the other half of my soul."

"You will not own mine."

Omne raised an eyebrow. "But—surely you know that it is for sale? There is the question of letting Spock leave here alive."

Kirk was silent, feeling his stomach crawl, his legs tremble. Finally he said, "You would lose everything. Star Fleet would take you apart from one side, and the Empire from the other. There's no such thing as impregnability, given time. My Mr. Scott also doesn't quit. Nor—the Commander."

Omne shook his head. "Mr. Spock will make his speech, or he will not. In either case, in an excess of grief and despondency, he will fall upon his sword—or the Vulcan equivalent. The Commander might even be persuaded to do the Romulan version. Star-crossed lovers, this time, seeing the failure of all their hopes. That would be a lovely script. Or—I'll write you three others. I can produce bodies. We might, if you are very good, keep a recording. Take it out and—play it—on special occasions. And—put it away."

"You understand that I will kill you," Kirk said as flat fact.

"Oh, yes," Omne said. "The automatic machinery is programmed for that contingency. It will scarcely inconvenience me."

"Or kill myself," Kirk said, knowing the answer already in his bones.

"The programming covers that, too," Omne confirmed. "There's no exit."

"There is always a way out of a box," Kirk said, seeing none.

"I can keep you for a thousand years. The Phoenix from the flames."

"If it takes me a thousand years, I will find the way to destroy your evil."

"Is it evil to offer eternal life?" Omne smiled distantly. "There was a time when I would have offered it to the galaxy. The time may come again. But I have seen in myself how it would be used."

"You are not the universe. You are a dark mirror. A bottomless pit. A black hole."

Omne drew himself up. "So are we all, Captain. *That* is what I can teach *you*. The other side of innocence. Your other half, which you imprison in a cage of virtue. Can't you feel it crying and raging to get out? Whimpering for the pleasure of being petted? Poor wolf. What gives it less right than virtue?"

"It is possible to be kind to—the wolf," Kirk said, with an effort, "without unleashing it at other throats." He put his hands on his thighs and straightened his shoulders. "Don't give me cop-outs, Omne, or excuses for evil. State your details. Name your price. I'll name mine. Spock—and his price. The Commander into the bargain."

"You would be willing to see Spock go free—with your—other, and willing never to see Spock again? You would stay with me for that?"

Kirk felt his jaw set. "Not—willing," he said. "I would grudge even—the other—the life that should have been mine. But he must have it if I can't. Spock is not to see me die—twice. You have me. I'll fight, but you want that. I'll stay—and see you damned."

Omne grinned. "Good! That also I wanted to learn. Yes, I'll have you, fighting—and I want that. You will learn to acknowledge me as your natural master. You'll learn to bend your stiff neck. You will be my final hostage against Spock, and he against you." He moved closer. "You are on your knees, but not to me. You will kneel and bow and beg for Spock."

Kirk smiled without amusement. "Only to be reminded that you are not a man of honor?"

"Perhaps," Omne said smoothly, "but with the certainty that you will see him die if you don't."

Kirk rose to his knees without a word, finding his face too close to the big man, but arching back a little and bowing his head. "I beg for Spock," he said easily, stressing the ease.

The gloved hands clenched into his hair, jerking his head up, pulling his chest against the corded thighs, his face almost against the great body.

Omne's face was the face of the wolf, the beast—the face of jungle and night. "Now beg for yourself. I am alpha here, and you will—now—yield."

One big hand twisted his head down and forward and the other ran down the back of his neck, feeling it cord and crackle with the resistance.

"Yield," the low voice snarled. "Let it happen."

Very suddenly Kirk released every muscle, letting the power of the big hands smash his forehead down into the target his knee had missed.

A roar, and as the giant doubled and the hands threatened to snap Kirk's neck, Kirk's arms caught tree-trunk legs at suddenly bending knees and toppled the hulk over backwards to the floor.

This time the giant fell heavily and was stunned, writhing. Kirk heaved himself forward with an abandonment of caution into the arms which could crush him, but going for the target again with his knee and with his hands for the throat and eyes. Omne flung him off and halfway across the room to smash against a wall. He could barely haul himself to his feet against the wall.

But the giant was rising again with a terrible vitality.

Murder was in the black eyes now, beyond mistake. Slow murder after much screaming.

Well, Kirk thought, that was what he had bought and paid for.

Spock's freedom, and his own.

It seemed the only way to buy both. He would not be the final hostage. Now it remained only to goad the dark fury.

Kirk gathered himself, using white fury against the pain, and dashed in, rapier against broadsword, with a quick stabbing punch, and out again, narrowly evading the slashing blind reply which tried to catch him.

He must not be caught, not until it would be killing, and he must not let the giant regain his mental balance.

Spock's freedom, he told himself like a prayer, and danced tauntingly again. Whatever this cost the Vulcan, it would free him to act. Whatever the difference, no replica would ever be quite the same to him as—the original. Nothing which happened to a replica would be quite the same. He could spare Spock that. And himself.

Even if Omne did not lie and the automatic machinery were already set for Kirk—which Kirk doubted that it was, so soon—but if it was, even if it would seem to him—to his successor—that death was scarcely an inconvenience, still it would not be quite the same.

In some sense there would still be old-fashioned death, his old enemy, and now perhaps a friend.

Curious how hard it was to feel that. Illogical.

Omne rushed him and he vaulted half-over the big man's shoulder, bull-dancer against bull.

Kirk had no illusions. The giant would regain sight and speed and precision in a moment. Kirk could not beat him. And the uncanny strength, the vicious imagination, could cause the Human body pain beyond its capacity to endure.

And the soul, also. Humiliation. A sickness of soul which could be felt through the body.

At some point he would beg abjectly, and for himself.

No illusions. Tough universe. It could be done to a man, any man. He had always known that it could be done to him. He had been very lucky.

And here his luck ran out.

One last hand to play. Raise and call with the last stack of chips. Pay the forfeit.

He had always known that there were things worth dying for.

He must learn now that there was something which he could not bear, which he would die not to have to bear.

Kirk ducked a sudden chop to his neck, rolled quickly away and to his feet.

And straightened very slowly.

So. His body knew it, then, if his mind did not. That chop of the massive hand would have killed, and quickly. It was the death he had courted, and he would not stand still for it.

In the end, then, he would choose life and bear what he had to bear. He would even bear what it would cost the Vulcan, as Spock would.

He felt his head lift with a sudden pride.

And he saw Omne stop, his black eyes reading the decision in the lifting head and the eyes that met his.

There was sight now in Omne's black eyes, and control, and a sudden glint of savage laughter which was both admiration and envy—a wish to possess some element of soul he did not own and to own the man who did—to punish the man who had the effrontery to own it.

The gloved hands dropped to the gunbelt and

slowly drew it off, drew the heavy leather strap
through the loop of the holster, tossed the holstered
gun carelessly aside to a couch—stressing no need to
use it, no need to fear that it could be used against its
owner.

Omne doubled the black strap and cracked the doubled end into a gloved palm with a sound like the
snap of doom.

So that was how it would begin, Kirk thought, feeling the dryness in his throat and refusing to swallow.

But Omne smiled, the smile reaching the black
eyes, underlining all of the possibilities. Then he
tossed the belt after the gun. "No," he said. "That does
not belong to the jungle." He began to strip off the
black gloves. "Nothing which does not will touch you,
and you will wish that it had been that simple." He
tossed the gloves after the belt, flexing the massive,
muscled, long-fingered hands. "Have you ever cried,
Captain, since you were a child?"

"No," Kirk said, somehow wanting this man to know
it. When Edith died, Miramanee—no, worse than
cried, possibly, but no. Other times— No.

Omne nodded. "Men don't cry, Captain. Curious
how widespread the necessity of that lesson is."

"Necessity? Or error?"

"Both," Omne said. "The alpha male must protect,
defend, cannot afford to cry. The jungle knows, but
we must learn. We must choose when we choose the
hard path. It is harder for us because we *can* cry."

Even Vulcans can, Kirk thought. And why not? But
was that it? Was it the alpha choice? Was that why he
never had, never could? "Doesn't matter," he said
aloud. "We choose what we choose."

"The choice can be broken," Omne said, "for—any
man."

"For *you*," Kirk said with sudden certainty.

"Once," Omne answered, the black eyes clearing to
the final depth again. "And now—for you."

"Not by this. *I* choose."

Omne shook his head. "Oh, no. You could bear to

choose to cry, as you could choose to beg—for Spock, for your choice, for others. Not for yourself. There will be no choice here. You will cry—for yourself—like a child, like a woman, and not be able to stop, and know that you have broken."

"No," Kirk said flatly—and then felt the unbidden amendment coming. "Not if I can help it."

Omne laughed. "*That* is the point, Captain. There is the point beyond help or endurance. You will cry—and then you will beg. You will know the real right of the man who can best you and master you."

"I'll see you in Hell first," Kirk said.

The laugh rumbled again. "Captain, this *is* Hell."

And then Omne came for him, this time with the speed which could not be matched—and making it look lazy, relaxed, even—playful.

Kirk dodged—and the black figure was already where he dodged.

Omne cuffed him lazily, great bear cuffing troublesome cub.

The blow caught only his shoulder, padded muscle which would take any ordinary blow. But he felt agony shoot through his body and he was slammed across the room, unable to catch himself. He slammed against the sharp metal corner of a cabinet, and it tore a gash across his back as he fell.

He got up slowly and turned to face the man again, ready to go at it again with all the Star Fleet and gutter-fighting skills he could still muster, but he knew already that he had lost. It remained only to keep on taking it to the last.

He caught a glimpse of horrified faces in the viewscreen, watching in helpless agony. But he had eyes only for Omne.

See him in Hell.

CHAPTER VIII

Spock ducked blindly into an alcove, slammed his hands flatly into the wall, and fought for control. He could not follow this, could not permit himself to follow it, while he must act for Kirk's life.

He fought to close down the link to the mere thread of contact, not to this wild and ravening torrent of emotion.

Kirk's own emotion Spock might have borne—the doomed courage which could be read in the fine face. But the link was to the—other—the other Kirk. Spock's— He hardly knew what to call him. James. He had started to make it James; he would have to make it James.

'James!' he called.

But James was shouting at Omne through the viewscreen, finally unable to bear his helplessness to stop what it showed.

He jerked to sudden awareness of the expansion of the link, an awareness Spock had retained the strength to shield him from since it happened.

'Spock?' he faltered, almost saying it aloud, closing his eyes against the viewscreen to focus on the inner call.

'That's right, James. Keep them closed. Help me to—withdraw. I must get to him.'

'You've seen—?'

'Through your eyes, your—feelings. From when Omne and the Commander came to you. The strong

59

emotion triggered the link. It was not your fault. My apologies.'

James was stricken. 'Oh, God, Spock. You can't have— How could you stand—?' He took a breath, with effort. 'He's—alive, Spock. Focus on that.' The effort came through again. 'Get to him. Where are you?'

'On my way. There was no time for subtlety. I "clobbered" a guard . . .'

The mind-touch dissolved into a ripple of quicksilver laughter—painfully, but the Human couldn't resist it. He always loved it when his Vulcan broke form. 'You appropriated the accoutrements,' James divined, flashing the Vulcan a small, swift vision of Spock in black jeans, silk shirt, antique boots with spurs. Hat? No hat. No need to hide the ears this time. 'Fascinating,' James remarked in Spock's manner, reaching for the trace of humor to steady himself, as Spock had wanted.

'Utilitarian.' Spock registered Vulcan approval for the steadiness. 'I have reached the maze, but must move carefully to maintain the guard's character. There are too many other guards. The turbo-lifts are off, apparently for security. You must stay where you are, even when the door yields.'

Spock felt the other's refusal, the effort to mask it, not to argue. There was the sound of a blow ringing on flesh, and the impact registered in James's flesh, and came through to Spock. Was it imagination? No. Some singular kind of—resonance? Some species of link to the too-similar body, too well-matched mind? James had been feeling more and more as if he were with Kirk's body from the first contact of the fight. Now James's eyes snapped open to see Kirk reeling from the blow, and James came close to reeling, too. He fought for balance, fought the agony, finally fought his eyes closed again to block the sight.

'That is another reason why you must not try to move,' Spock flashed sternly. 'You must help me to tune down the link so that *I* can.'

Once again James gave obedience—to that last order at least. He threw himself into the effort, not fully knowing how, but helping. He fought for emotional control, the Human's own kind. It was hard, very hard for him. He fought for withdrawal. That was even harder. But he was trying. Making it. Making it perhaps better than his Vulcan. Slowly James was screening out the terror of the flesh as he had screened out the sight of the eyes.

Spock focused on the need to move, denying the need to feel, to see, to know, to be—with. He was narrowing everything down to the central vision of a tunnel opening before him. Narrowing, with the effort of his life. Now, when it counted to be a Vulcan.

At the edge of the narrowing, Spock felt hands shaking his shoulders—whose shoulders? Kirk's? Which Kirk? James? A slim hand slapped a face, and it registered on Spock's face, but he knew then that the Commander had slapped James.

' "Captain!" ' The woman's voice, as from a distance. ' "The door, Captain. Now. James T. Kirk! Jim! My—Kirk—" ' She slapped him harder.

Spock pulled out as James Kirk opened his eyes and caught the Commander's wrist. Spock must leave—James—to her now. There was no time—

Spock found his eyes looking at a blank wall inches from his face. His mind was—yes—clear. Only a slender cable of a link remained.

Then he felt a heavy hand impacting against his jaw, crushing flesh against bone, this time one fraction of force from snapping the neck. No, not Spock's own neck—Kirk's. Jim Kirk's. Spock felt the shocking vulnerability of the Human—the power of the black giant against that more delicate flesh.

And then Spock knew that he was going to feel it all, as James would—as—Jim—would. James could screen the sight out of the link, but not the singular resonance, growing stronger now with Kirk's agony. It was beyond tuning out.

A slap rocked Spock's head again, but he set Vulcan

muscles against it, stopping the movement down to a convulsive jerk. Yes, he would feel it, but he was a Vulcan. It was beyond his capacity to want to tune it out.

But he could see now and he could move.

He moved.

CHAPTER IX

The Commander took her Kirk's face in her hands
as if she could soothe his cheeks, which bore white
imprints of hands. Had her hands done that? She had
thought she had been gentle enough even for a Human. This Human.

Where had he been?

He was here now. Trembling, but here.

"The door," she repeated, turning his face to it,
away from the screen, averting her own eyes. There
was work to do. "Jim—?" she said tentatively.

"Call me—James," he said distantly. And then
brought his eyes into focus on her face. "I'm sorry.
Let's go."

She started to release him, but the cheeks tightened
convulsively under her hands to the sound of a heavy
blow. Every muscle in his body— She held him
against it.

She felt her eyes widening. She had seen him in
glimpses while she worked on the door, seen his helpless rage turn to trancelike absorption, seen the faint
movements of body language backing the other's
fight.

But he was feeling it in truth, in his own body.

"Are you—able?" she said, shocked.

He set himself with monumental effort, as if drawing on some strength he did not own. There was another slap and he reeled, but caught himself. "I'll
move. Let's *move!*"

"Behind me," she said, leveling the nearly exhausted sidearm and impacting the heel of her boot solidly against the last of the lock to snap it.

She followed the motion of the kick through into the candled room, prepared to fire but finding the candles guttering out in emptiness.

So, the doubled or tripled guard would be out in the corridor. Count on Omne for that. He knew they would try to come.

The last remnants of the weapon's charge which she had saved might or might not get them through the first contingent—might get them no more than a dozen yards.

She saw no chance, in fact, of reaching Kirk.

But she could not tell this one that he could not try.

"Crawling with guards," the Human said quietly.

She nodded.

This door, she had noted, did not lock. It opened out, in fact, in the antique fashion which Omne maintained throughout much of the place.

She turned the knob silently and burst out, feeling the door slam into hard flesh.

She mowed the guards down without word or hesitation. The sidearm's stun effect accounted for four before she cut it off, jammed it in the holster, and went for the two shaken ones behind the door with her feet and the edges of her hands.

It was over before the man behind her could get past her and into the action. She bent and collected two of the ancient guns, jammed them in her belt, indicating one for him. "Useless until we reach him," she said. "They make too much noise."

She saw him looking a little stunned, but she turned toward the turbo-lift.

He caught her shoulder. "No turbo-lifts."

She raised an eyebrow. How would he know?

"Spock," he said. She nodded and turned him toward the emergency slide-poles and ladder tubes Omne had cheerfully pointed out to her on his guided tour. He had been proud of his miserable maze, confident that it could block any effort to break it. Letting her know that. And now—

A dozen levels down and an unknown horizontal distance through unknown turnings. U-27-E-14.

She kept her hand on the Human's arm, feeling him fighting against turning his attention inward—winning, but losing at certain moments when he could not suppress the reaction of his body.

She locked her hand into the stretchy velvet tunic and the wide hip-band as she stepped off before him to catch the slide-pole.

For an instant his startled eyes said damn it, he could look out for himself. Then he countered the argument himself and caught the pole a little above her, letting his legs circle her thighs around the pole, and locking one arm around the pole, one around her, until she felt that she had a more secure hold than the thin material but did not let it go. Was there another Human male in the galaxy who would not have delayed, defending his pride? She kicked her foot out of the stop-stirrup and let them slide.

And in fact he even let her Romulan muscles take the greater share of the strain of braking against gravity in the long slide—a slide designed for Romulan muscles and not for his, though he might have managed it on a normal day. At need, he would have managed it today, if it killed him. But it might have.

She counted the levels mostly by feel and caught the stop-stirrup with her foot, wondering whether it would have broken his ankle. Possibly. The heavier gravity here was more like Romulan or Vulcan, too, not meant for his fragile strength.

But he was quick and active in swinging off onto the level and he caught her hand and pulled her up and after him.

She let him set the direction. It was as good as any other. The tour had showed her that the doors appeared to be numbered normally, but in fact were numbered by no system known to man—or mathematics. Forty-seven unblushingly followed eighty-three and led to 16-C. As far as she could tell, only the level numbers counted and made sense.

It was an astute security system, really. A man who had business there would memorize the relevant parts of the maze. The rooms could be referred to by number for the turbo-lift, and the computer would select the nearest stop. But with the lifts off, a stranger could spend hours checking every door, even to find a known number.

Hardly a road map.

She had not thought it wise to say so.

That was doubtless one of Omne's little laughs. He could have removed the number from Kirk's door if he had not wanted to create, at some point, precisely that hope.

She wondered if Spock had noticed the numbering on his way to the candled room—under that stress. But, yes, almost certainly, with that Vulcan mind. Now the Human must have told Spock the number. Some link—although how they were managing that at a distance she could not fathom. But the Vulcan would have known that the hope was false. Where was Spock now, knowing it?

The Human was just finding it out, turning to her with another look she hoped not to see again.

She nodded with effort and freed her left hand from his to take his arm. Nothing to do but look. He staggered from some blow and she steadied him.

A dark figure rounded a corner in front of them, and her eyes determined that it was not Spock while her gun hand flashed to the sidearm. The guard dropped and the weapon tingled in her hand, signalling emptiness.

CHAPTER X

It was not working, Spock concluded, letting light-ning calculation click over at the sub-thought level one last time, on the hypothesis of some hidden pat-tern to the numbering system. None. Null. True ran-domness.

It was possible that the only hope was to capture the turbo-lift system, reinstate it, and order delivery at the nearest lift position.

Time.

Time already had run out. The agony was more than mere pain now. Defeat. Loss. Hopelessness. Spock struggled to see and to keep moving.

He had permitted himself—illogical hopes.

Among them that there would be some extension of the directionality of the link through the strange re-sonsance.

But there was not.

He could follow the movements of—James.

But only the feelings of Jim.

James. Suddenly Spock became aware that James was leading the Commander, his movements shifting from bafflement to purpose—tentative, groping—but purpose. As if James were following the most fragile gossamer thread—but following, and leading.

Spock sighed. The resonance, then, did offer some clue, not to him but to James. It would lead James to

Kirk and the link would lead Spock to James. Too late, but not too late to kill.

Spock set off quartering across the level, trying to anticipate the other's direction, afraid to reach for more contact for fear of snapping the gossamer thread.

CHAPTER XI

The Commander stayed silent and supported the arm of the man at her side. He did not look at the numbers. She doubted that he saw anything. His body seemed numbed even beyond pain, not capable of feeling her touch, but allowing himself to be steered by main force to keep from running into walls. And it was just as well that she had the main force to steer him.

But it was he who had the direction.

She did not know what he was doing or how he was doing it. But she followed.

They were angling now. He was trying to walk through the left-hand wall. Warp him around the corner gently now.

Suddenly she saw the tears burst from his eyes, his already heaving breath catch in a sob. Astonishment in the face, and shame, utter defeat—and still some kind of resistance, setting his teeth against words which screamed to come out with the sobs and were held back. She knew that she was not seeing the face of the man beside her.

But the man she held set his jaw, too, and kept moving, blindly, tears streaming, around one corner after another.

Then at the end of a long stretch of corridor, on the big swinging doors at its end, she saw the number.

She leaned him against a wall, left him, and broke into a run.

There was only one guard.

His back was to her and his eye was glued to a crack between the doors.

She hit him under the ear with the edge of her hand, telling herself that it was only necessary to knock him out. She suspected that she had broken his neck.

She saw over her shoulder that her Kirk was lurching after her, trying somehow to see.

She pulled both revolvers.

The hairline crack between the doors seemed to show light from top to bottom except for a rather slender bolt. She smashed with the boot heel again and went through the bursting doors.

She plunged straight in, and for an instant her eyes would not find the men. Then, halfway across the big room, in a tumble of furniture, Kirk on his knees in a kind of crumpled, tattered, bloody heap—Omne standing over him. The giant's back was to her, and something in the set of his shoulders was the essence of arrogance and triumph, before he reacted to the sound of the swinging doors, saw her over his shoulder, and flung himself down on a Kirk struggling to rise.

Her right hand had come up to shoot Omne in the back and it followed him down, but in the split instant of distrusting the strange weapon's aim so near the Human, she had lost the chance. The two men were intertangled and down among the furniture, and then Omne had locked an arm around Kirk and was scuttling crabwise to one side, dragging the Human in front of him toward the cover of a big couch.

No chance for a shot.

She ran, leaping over furniture, seeing too late that it was the couch which held the holstered gun as Omne's arm snaked over the back to grab the weapon.

A bullet whipped through her hair as she dived for the deck and tossed off a snap shot at the aiming arm. For a snap shot it was close, and she thought that it burned the black silk. The arm jerked back and she rolled, almost reaching the cover of a desk, but looking back, hoping to see that her Kirk had not reached the doors yet.

But he had, and he had not taken cover.

He was lurching and weaving in a low rush toward the area behind the couch.

She vaulted up and rushed the couch, leaping over it in time to see the tattered Kirk raise a feeble hand to spoil Omne's aim at the rushing Kirk.

Omne swore and cuffed his Kirk with the heel of his gun hand.

She still could get no shot, and Omne had gained several yards under cover of the couch while her Kirk was making his berserker rush.

And now she saw the big man's objective as he rolled into it—the drop-hole of a slide-pole, opening behind a panel which had slid aside at Omne's touch.

He had Kirk slung on one hip, his left arm around Kirk's waist, and the gun still in his right hand. She saw Omne's right elbow catch the pole, but could not see down into the hole to see whether the big legs had caught and held with their awkward burden.

For a long moment she expected to hear screams and a long sounding of falling.

But, no.

And as her Kirk reached the hole and stepped out into space, she expected it again.

She was a step away from him and too late.

But she saw his arms catch as she reached the hole and saw the three figures diminishing down into further depths, but not at the speed of falling. If he could hold—

She started to swing around the pole after him, but the turn brought her to see Spock, already charging across the room, his eyes hollow with the knowledge that he was much too late.

She saw a renegade Romulan guard, bowled off his feet by the Vulcan and aiming at Spock's back.

She shot the Romulan down without hesitation and with some satisfaction.

She started again to step off onto the pole as Spock reached her. But she looked down and saw the pole— empty.

Any one of uncounted levels, each a labyrinth as tortuous as this one. There would be no guide. Perhaps a long, slow search for a trail of blood, for a battered figure with the haunted eyes wet with the tears of a Starship Captain. For another figure in white velvet—probably also to be found in blood.

There was perhaps only one man in the universe whom she would permit herself to look to for help.

She looked to him now.

And found the help even in the tortured eyes.

"I can find them," Spock said with control. "If— they—live," the torture added in the Vulcan's voice. "Come," he said to her, and stepped off onto the pole.

She followed.

CHAPTER XII

James Kirk limped on an ankle wrenched almost to breaking and on bare thighs scalded to blood by the friction of the pole, but he barely noticed that or his raw scalded hands for the pain from the other Kirk's body, which throbbed still in his own.

And he fought to keep the other's pain, for it was his guide.

They had dropped—God knew how many levels. Possibly twice the first drop. But he had seen where Omne left the pole. He had caught that stop-stirrup as he had seen the Commander do, but his foot was dragged out of it by the force. That left him clawing and catching the edge with his hands, and when he could look, Omne was out of sight with his burden.

Oh God, he was going to get very damn tired of this place.

He lurched raggedly along the halls, scrubbing at his eyes with the backs of his hands, mostly managing to keep from crashing into walls.

He could have used the Commander.

He could use Spock.

But that could not be.

That could never really be.

The right was not his. The friendship. All the years before—and to come. The agonies and the little private jokes. The shared looks speaking volumes in a familiar silence.

The right. It was the right of the other, who had

just learned the meaning of Hell for that right. He had earned it again, and it had always been his.

The link, for all its agony, was still full of the subdued note of the single fact which had been singing in the Vulcan's mind, beyond shielding and beyond the need for words: *Jim alive.*

Not all the Vulcan's generosity would ever erase the difference. He had spoken the name of James.

James. He was James. He had to be James.

But damn it, he was also Jim. Always had been. And—he grudged even—the other—the life which should have been his.

He heard the echo of—Jim's—voice saying, "But he must have it if I can't."

Was there no difference?

Did—James—have *that*? Whatever said those words— and paid the cost?

James lurched around a corner. Down there somewhere he told himself.

He was about to find out.

CHAPTER XIII

Jim Kirk scrubbed at his eyes and tried to see, tried to breathe against the sobbing that racked him in uncontrollable spasms, tried somehow to ease the intolerable mass of pain that was his whole body.

It was only a little worse where the big arm crushed him against the massive chest, carrying him now like a child, the single arm looped around his chest and under his thighs, balancing him on one hip, while the other arm reached for something. He saw it find some hidden spot on a plain panel on a corridor wall. The panel slid back and in, then aside. Omne stepped through and turned to close it.

They were moving into some inner labyrinth, Kirk saw. There were tiny corridors, branching.

Fight. No one would ever find him here. Fight, he told himself.

And he knew suddenly that he could not.

Could not.

It was not in him, not even the will to fight. He could never remember a time when that had left him, that willingness to get up and make one more effort. There had been moments when muscle had failed, but never *that*. It was gone now, as if it had never been.

Abruptly he swung a leaden arm at the heathen-idol face. When muscle failed, will, nerve, guts—there still had to be something.

Omne only let the blow roll off the side of his head. And he looked down and smiled almost benignly, then finished closing the panel.

A sob racked Kirk's chest and he fought then just not to close his eyes and huddle, not to crawl off into some corner of his mind and never look out of his eyes again, never try to meet the eyes of a man.

If you close your eyes, he told himself, you're finally finished. Don't think. You don't have to think. Don't feel. You can't let yourself feel. Just look out of the eyes. Omne plunged into the inner labyrinth and Kirk made himself look at the way. It would not be a way out for him, but it was a way to keep himself looking.

They came to branches and to some kind of baffle walls of paneling blocking the passages. Omne pressed at a spot on each panel, the fingers of his free hand twisting in a pattern to touch hidden electronic studs imbedded in the paneling. Another touch closed them behind.

Almost idly Kirk noted the pattern.

No, he must not permit himself to hope. Hope could be used against him. Had been; it was hope which had broken him. Hope, and the playing on it, and the slow, unrelenting destruction of it.

Omne stepped through a panel into a big room. Old books lined the walls.

A study, Kirk thought, as Omne put him down on the couch.

The big arms swung him down with surprising gentleness and rolled him onto his face. But he bolted up onto his side and onto an elbow, trying to ignore the convulsive shaking of his arm.

Look up and meet the eyes, meet them, damn it, or you never will.

The black eyes looked down, and something in them approved the man whose eyes could still meet them.

Omne nodded then, and turned and busied himself with the air of a man who had reached haven. He moved into an alcove and was back out momentarily, with the black jumpsuit smoothed down, rolling up a torn sleeve to reveal a bullet burn. It seemed to be the only damage he had suffered. And he had replaced the lost holster, dropped the gun into its twin.

He moved toward the couch.

"Why here?" Kirk said, discovering that he could, after all, speak.

Omne raised an eyebrow as if surprised that he could or would. "My safe-house," he answered easily, as if he had no secrets left to hide from the eyes which could still meet his. "No other living soul knows that it is here. It needs no locks but silence and concealment. If the planet fell, the fortress, the underground, only a foot-by-foot measurement would find this inner complex. We could live here for decades on stored supplies."

It came to Kirk suddenly through the calm words: Omne was that afraid of dying. His whole life was built around not dying. He had invented immortality, not to preserve someone loved, not really for a galactic purpose, not even for the pleasure of tormenting Kirk, but as a last defense against the fear of death.

"We?" Kirk said, realizing something else. "But why bring me to your last refuge?"

"You will be safe here." The black eyes glowed with a certain satisfaction.

"But why even run?" Kirk asked savagely. "From—a woman—and an unarmed man." Twist the knife. Never mind that the Romulan cavalry looked pretty good. "You could have shot it out. Guards would come running. Were you scared of the ferocious opposition?" Make him admit the fear.

But Omne only looked startled, as if trying to trace down the reason for something which had struck him as self-evident. "I—" He hesitated, but the mood of self-revelation held. "I did not want you in the line of fire."

Kirk felt an odd jolt on some level he couldn't even name. Or—wouldn't. Perhaps somewhere on the level of what he was refusing to name, even to himself. Let it be blunt, brute fact.

But this—

He had snapped out the questions as fury, as re-lease, half-hoping to goad an admission of cowardice.

But what frightened him was to learn that the big man was not a coward. The man was pathological about death, he knew it, he didn't let it stop him.

And yet— "At—any other time," Kirk said carefully, "your only thought would have been for your life— or—some game."

Omne smiled with the look of being understood. "Yes," he said.

"And—this time—it didn't even occur to you."

Omne nodded gravely. "No."

The jolt he had—it was something very like pride, Kirk realized, and was shocked on some deeper level. It was as if this man had said: What I did to you, what I made you show of what you are, makes you worth more than my life.

And it was as if that could matter to Kirk.

But that *was* what the man had said.

And it did matter.

In some terrible way, it did matter.

"But—you *did* break me," he said against the tight agony in his chest. "I did—cry."

"You cried," Omne said. "You didn't break."

"How—do you know?" Kirk blurted. How do you know—when I *don't?* he choked back into his throat, but he thought that Omne heard it.

"You never—begged," Omne said.

Didn't I? Somehow he still stopped the words in his throat. It could not be for this man to know. It could not be for Kirk to ask this man for confirmation, for— comfort.

"No," Omne said, answering the unspoken question, giving the confirmation, perhaps even the comfort.

But wasn't it begging? Kirk thought. The crying and the words which had screamed in his mind, even if he had somehow stopped them at his throat. Hadn't he cried because he could not speak, would not—and wasn't that a kind of begging, too?

No. He answered himself this time. No, it was not the same.

But the knowledge did not seem to help. Something had still broken, and he was not sure what. But—there was also something which had not.

Hold to that.

"No," he said. "I didn't beg. Does it matter?"

Omne nodded. "I never wanted to break you."

Kirk laughed harshly, finding breath for it somewhere. "You did your damndest!"

"Certainly. How else would I know that I never can?" He smiled. "Or you—that you never will?"

"You said—any man can be broken."

Omne shook his head. "I said—any man can cry. Until he does, he doesn't know whether that will break him."

"And if it doesn't." Kirk said bitterly, "then—you try again?"

Another shake of the massive head. "I will not have to try again. And—will never want to."

Kirk frowned. "Never want to break me to play beta to your alpha?"

Omne's smile held a hint of the wolf, but the eyes were grave, almost gentle. "Ah, but don't you know? That was what you did lose tonight when you decided to live. But it wasn't—breaking. You know what kind of victory it was."

Omne smiled at him as if he had invented him, and said, "That is why a thousand years will not be long enough."

Kirk felt his breath catch sharply. The black eyes glowed as if with banked flames.

The big man turned abruptly and took something from a drawer, a long, slender silver tube. Kirk thought finally that it might be some odd kind of spray can.

Omne came back to the couch.

"Turn over," he ordered.

Kirk tried not to flinch away, tried not to ask. But he did ask. "What—what are you—?"

"I am going to fix your back."

"*What*—?" Kirk found himself laughing on the edge of hysteria, the tears threatening to come again. "While your Wild West plays shoot-'em-up over our heads? While your ally and your—replica—get hunted through the corridors? While the delegates wait and Spock waits, somewhere. And *you* are going to fix my back?"

"Among other things," Omne said. "Turn over."

"Go to hell."

"As you please, Captain. I can begin on the front."

"I don't want it. Go tend to your knitting."

"If I do, it will be tended much more effectively. I will get the Commander. And my replica. The Wild West will, too. But it may take longer. That would give them some sporting chance. Spock will have a little longer to stall before his performance. They can all wait, while I restore the original."

"You'd need a sickbay—not a spray can," Kirk said bitterly, and knew that it was concession.

Omne sat down on the edge of the couch. "I *have* a sickbay—in the can," he said. His hands ripped free the last fragments which held Kirk's shirt, not asking permission. "A growth-forcer," he continued dispassionately in the tone of a scientific dissertation. "Local metabolic accelerator. Antiseptic. Anesthetic, with deep-pain extensors. Cleansing." His hands unfastened the belt which still held what was left of the tough Star Fleet uniform. Kirk started to protest, realized that it was no use. "In a few seconds, you will be free of pain. There are no broken bones or grave internal injuries. I was careful. In a few more minutes there will be delicate new flesh and skin, swelling will go down, bruises clear, cuts and contusions begin to mend. In a few hours—you will be good as new."

He finished with the clothes, boots and all, almost in the manner of a doctor. Kirk set his teeth and tried to take it as medical, wishing devoutly for Bones McCoy, then retracting the wish. Better Bones didn't have to deal with this.

Omne picked up the spray can again. "This place is, among other things, probably the finest research laboratory in the galaxy. You would be surprised to learn how many first-rate scientists from how many planets find refuge here. They are on holiday today in honor of the conference. Some of them are delegates."

Kirk was surprised, and let it register a little. He had seen the place only as a great, empty setting for Omne's evil.

"You would be shocked to learn how many new products we market through how many channels." Omne hefted the can. "It pays the rent. This one happens to be one of mine. My—public—lab is not far from here. The private one—" he shrugged and smiled. "Lie down."

Kirk caught his lip between his teeth. It was not that he wanted to obey, he told himself. It was only that his arm really wouldn't hold him any longer. It was for the Commander, for—the other. Even for Spock. Buy time. That was it.

But he knew that he believed Omne even in his boast about his power for good. He knew why the man needed to make that boast now in the face of the evidence of his power for evil and to the man who had felt all his power.

Kirk knew. He knew this man very well.

With sudden, numbing force it came home to Kirk what had broken, and why he had cried.

He had been hurt before, terrified before. He had been terrified by experts. Tortured. Faced with more than he could take. It had never broken him.

The physical pain was as bad as any he had ever taken, but it was not worse.

But this time he had met his match.

His breath caught and he made himself say it. No. It was worse than that. Omne had said it, and it was true.

This man had played with him, overreaching him in every direction—mind, body, will. So easily. Lazily. Beyond possibility of resistance.

And Kirk had almost felt some ancient jungle law telling him that this man *was* his natural master, this man had, even, the right.

It was what Omne had wanted him to feel and why the giant had done it.

He could see it now in the black eyes, see them reading him, too, and knowing that he felt it.

"No," he said aloud. "I do not live in the jungle. No man is my master."

"I am," Omne said. "By the most ancient law of all, I am. *That* was what you could not take."

"I—took it," Kirk said with bleak pride.

Omne nodded. "And you did not surrender. But the jungle in you did. You feel it now. You want to obey. You will always want to, and always want to fight. But you know me. You know me as master. Sometime in a thousand years you will find that compliance has become obedience—and that you never knew the moment when it happened." He smiled. "Perhaps this moment."

"No," Kirk whispered, but he saw the thousand years in Omne's eyes.

"No?" Omne said softly. "But you will comply now. You will tell yourself that it is for others, but it will be for yourself. Or you will find the honesty to know it. Lie down now. You do not have to look at me."

Omne's hand caught the back of Kirk's neck, lightly, but turning his face down. And it was too much. The quivering arm would not hold. Perhaps—something else would not hold.

Kirk let his shoulders down, let himself bury his face. Yes, just let it happen. God, he was so tired.

He lifted his head and turned his face to one side against the knotted neck muscles and Omne's light touch to look up and meet the eyes. It was all he could do, but it was enough.

"Not just yet," he whispered. "See you in hell first."

Omne smiled with that look of having invented him. "That's my original," he said. "I could not have chosen better."

Kirk felt the odd jolt of pride again, but set himself against it. He would not let that matter, either. No, it would matter, but it would not stop him. He would set hate against it and control and cool logic.

It would be a long thousand years.

Omne released his neck and took up the spray can.

The spray drifted down onto Kirk's back, a coolness of flowing mist and drifting foam, cooling flame. Then Omne's hands were busy through the coolness, easing cuts together where flesh had split over bone, smoothing the foam to where it was most needed.

Kirk set his teeth against the touch, and against fighting it.

But he felt pain die slowly down the length of his body, finally even in deep bruises and final knotted lumps of resistance. The relief was almost an agony in itself, and he felt himself clutching for the last of the pain like an anchor. He was beginning to—drift. The shock he had held at bay was catching up with him. The last of the sobs were dying down to the tiny jerks of a cried-out child sinking into sleep. The Starship Captain's eyes were dry now, but he was crying himself to sleep. At least Spock did not know. The Vulcan would never know . . .

Kirk flickered his eyes open for a second to look at Omne. The big man's rough-carved face was almost gentle. So many facets to the man. So many faces. No one would ever find this place, and in a thousand years Kirk would not know all the faces. But he would remember always the face of the wolf . . .

CHAPTER XIV

The Commander was not accustomed to feeling helpless.

Her Kirk pressed the stained white velvet, the bloodstained hands, his face, against the blank wall. "I—can't—" he murmured, "I'm losing—I've lost—the signal."

His shoulders shuddered under Spock's hands, and the Vulcan's stoned-carved face set harder, but his voice was gentle, saying, "It's all right. It will be better for you now. For him."

The shaking figure pried itself away from the wall, twisted; the raw hands seized Spock's arms. "Better! The—pain—the feeling—gone. I've lost him. Don't you understand? We can't get to him, even now. And now Omne could take him anywhere."

"I know," Spock said very quietly, looking down into the tormented eyes as if to give support.

They were locked away from her in some world she could not reach, had been, since Spock had led her to the one he called James. She could not quite bring herself to adopt the name. How, really, had they exchanged it? And what had it meant to them? Spock had not spoken it but once, minutes ago, when they found—the other—trying to get through a blank wall. There was evidently some kind of link still persisting. She did not think, somehow, that she liked that, although it had undoubtedly saved such sanity as remained to any of them by leading Spock to him. She

did not fully understand it, did not understand at all
the mechanism by which they both seemed to be feeling what Kirk felt. Spock controlled it better, but she
could see it in his rock-steady face, too. Yet the—
connection—did not seem to be through Spock.

They had checked the adjoining rooms, her Kirk
persistently indicating that he—felt—Kirk in a direction where it did not seem that he could be, and
which Spock could evidently not sense. They had
tried to check for secret panels, secret passageways,
with the helpless feeling that a secret hidden by
Omne could elude them for hours.

They had ducked guards.

And finally her Kirk had fetched up against the
blank wall again, going rigid, then whispering, "Some
kind of—medical—attention," but not relaxing. And
Spock had supported the rigid shoulders, also looking
like grim death.

Now he said, "James . . . "

But her Kirk's chin line was already firming, the
eyes steadying as if to return support, the hands
squeezing and releasing the Vulcan's arms. "Thank
you, Spock. Of course, we just have to get to him." He
turned to the wall appraisingly. "We know the direction right now. Omne presumably will be getting reor-
ganized in a moment—move him—rally the troops, whatever. Perhaps a time for direct action. Do you think
that a couple of Vulcanoids could start taking that
paneling apart?" He flashed a look at the Commander, including her in.

She stepped forward, casting a pointed look at his
raw hands, scalded on an ordinary slide-pole. "So long
as the Humanoid doesn't try to."

Spock touched the Human's shoulder aside with the
delicacy of moving a child, and slammed his fist
through the wall.

He stood frozen for a moment looking as if he had
been needing to do that for a long time. Then he put
his forearm in through the cleanly fractured hole in the

heavy composition paneling, hauled back on it, and pulled it free with a sound of fasteners snapping like the rattle of ancient weapons.

But there was only solid stone a few inches behind it. She started on the edge of the next sheet with not much less delicacy.

"That will do," Omne said, and they looked up to see him with a sudden arm around James Kirk's neck and a gun leveled at them past his waist.

He nodded pleasantly. "It is as simple as that," he said. "And it is just as well that I took a look at the monitor screens. Good afternoon, Mr. Spock. I observe the meaning of your word."

Spock freed his hand from the paneling and let it fall against the wall. There could be no question of trying to draw. "I have observed the meaning of yours."

"As a matter of fact," Omne said, "I gave you no word not to do anything which I have done—not even about 'damaged merchandise.' You made assumptions." He shrugged. "But then, *I* never claimed to be a man of honor."

"I—owe—no—honor—to—" Spock's voice caught further and then he spat it out with naked loathing, "—to what you are."

Omne raised an eyebrow. "Behold Vulcan control." He eased his forearm hold on James Kirk's throat a little, and slipped the arm down across the front of his shoulders. "However, I cannot say that I blame you. Interesting problem, Spock, which of us would have broken a word first, and to whom—and for whom. Did you have any intention of keeping yours to me—for this one?"

James Kirk's eyes suppressed any flicker of motion. "I will keep it now, for both of them," Spock said.

Omne shook his head. "That was not the question, Mr. Spock—nor the bargain. The galactic script for—one copy. Would you have made good on that—and will you?"

Spock met James Kirk's eyes. "My intention was to play out the script."

Omne must have felt a faint movement which the Commander's eyes could not detect. He looked down at the man he held. "That pleases you?"

"Spock plays them as he sees them," James Kirk said, his words for Omne, his eyes only for Spock. "He has never played me false."

"He has had precious little time," Omne said rather harshly. "You have no 'never' with him."

James Kirk straightened the tightly held shoulders further. "I have all that it is possible for me to have."

"Then let us find out what that is," Omne said grimly. He started to draw the Human closer against him and back down the hall toward an open door which led into a big lab. Omne wanted to be out of the way of stray guards, she thought, and followed helplessly, as did the Vulcan, while Omne continued with complete control. "The bets are still down, Spock. Mine stands. I will ignore the fact that the three of you have caused me certain inconveniences and doubtless damaged some guards. It is what they get paid for. You and the Commander may take this one, as agreed. The Commander can stay with him and supervise the—alterations—while you give your performance. In an hour I will beam the three of you to her ship—if you have any intention of honor."

"My intention," Spock said carefully, watching for any chance and seeing none, "was based on the slim chance that you would honor your word, and the greater chance that you would break it at some point, releasing me from mine. The damage done by a speech can be repaired. A life is irreplaceable—even now."

Omne chuckled, shepherding them into an open space in the big lab. "You do feel that about this one—even now? But that is the complete success of my process. The copy is so perfect that he is irreplaceable to you—even though I could make another. And do you speak of honoring your word, Spock? For him?"

"In fact, one owes no honor to force," Spock said. "You forfeited all rights in this matter from the beginning. But it is impossible for men to deal with each other, even under duress, especially under duress, if there is no word. Speech becomes noise. Yours is. Yours was always a crooked game, and now you have broken letter and spirit of any agreement—and every law of decency. All bets are off."

"Irrelevant, Mr. Spock, whether true or not. No bets are off. The question is, Do you want this one?"

"Both of them," Spock said.

"*That* you cannot have," Omne answered. "Apart from anything else, can you conceive of turning up with both of them—in the Romulan Empire?"

"I will undertake to solve that problem," the Commander said flatly.

Omne raised an eyebrow to her. "My dear, do you not think that that might be an embarrassment of riches, even for you?"

"I'll manage," she said.

Omne laughed. "Perhaps you could, at that. However—" He looked back to Spock. "The Commander can verify part of this. The—damages—to the—other merchandise—have been repaired. There is no pain now and no threat to his life, now or ever. He has accommodated to his situation. He is hostage for your dubious word for the next two hundred years. He chooses to live even in those circumstances. He is quite beyond your reach or finding, beyond anyone's but mine. Wherever you thought he was a moment ago, he is not now. However you found him here, you seem to have lost him now. Were you to kill me now where I stand, you would never reach the surface, and no one would ever reach him. There is food, water, air. He might last a hundred years. Alone."

"What of your boast that death would not inconvenience you?" the Commander said, filling it in for Spock. "The automatic machinery—set for you—and him?"

Spock did not look surprised.

Omne shrugged. "I might have lied. I am not a man of honor. If I didn't, then my death here or elsewhere, now or later, would only start the game again. If I did or didn't, you would never know it. Unless I so chose. My estate here is set up in trust in capable hands. It will run for a thousand years, perhaps forever, if I die or disappear." He raised the gun to his temple. "It may be that I could go now by still another exit, to join Kirk—or leave him alone. Would you care to chance it?"

"No," Spock said.

Omne laughed and dropped the gun into his holster. "Then you will not chance it in a thousand years."

The Commander considered. From a standing draw she could needle-beam a target considerably smaller than the part of the massive head showing above and beside her Kirk's. And her right-hand gun had fired true. Omne's argument went for Spock. Did it go for her? *Her* Kirk was here. She had not pledged "friends" with the other, only acted the friend. And wouldn't a true friend kill Omne for Kirk now? Wouldn't he a thousand times rather be alone? Truth or lie, this Omne dead would buy a little time to look. And when she thought the time was up, she could make these two go—if necessary at the point of a gun. Kirk might even want that. He deserved better. But there were her needs, too. And there was reality.

"No, Commander!"

She stopped her hand before it moved. Her Kirk had spoken in the voice of the Starship Captain. Her thought had crystallized almost faster than words. She had not thought that she had telegraphed it by the flicker of a muscle. Omne had not read it. But her Kirk had.

Spock looked at her.

Omne said, "Well, well, my dear," and pulled his gun again. "Mr. Spock, you will relieve Calamity Jane of the hardware. That is a disposal chute directly to your left."

Spock moved behind her to take her two guns, look-ing not at her but at James Kirk.

She was certain that for a long moment Spock con-templated some such decision as she had. He must re-gard her action as a kind of betrayal. And what was he to make of the Human's action in stopping her? Defense of the real Kirk—or betrayal of them all? Some game of his own? This Kirk was up to some-thing, and the Vulcan didn't like it.

But Omne's argument still went for the Vulcan.

Spock dropped three guns in the chute.

"Excellent, Mr. Spock," Omne said. "So much for Romulan honor—and possibly Human. However, you should thank the Human for your life, my dear. I would have outdrawn you."

"Conceivably," she said, "but you would still have been dead, and Spock and this Human alive."

Omne raised an eyebrow. "This one? You do not mention the other?"

"He, too," she said with effort.

"*He* is the point," the Human cut in. "There is a logic to this situation which you have all missed."

"Indeed?" Omne said. "Have you learned logic from Spock, Human?"

The Human shook his head and smiled fractionally at Spock. "Poker," he said. "I just dealt myself a hand." He twisted a little to look up at Omne. "Re-lease me and let me face you."

"*No*, James," Spock said with quiet urgency, as if he knew this man and that tone too well.

"I'm sorry, Mr. Spock," the Human said firmly, in the tone of command.

Omne raised an interested eyebrow and smiled, then released the human, giving him a little whirl out to form the third point of a triangle. "Place your bet."

The Human caught himself and straightened. "A two-handed game," he said, jerking his head to indi-cate drawing Omne aside to talk privately.

Omne smiled indulgently. "If you have some thought of throwing yourself on my gun, so that they can try to take me with muscle, I assure you that you overestimate Mr. Spock, and the Commander is not in the picture."

"I would not count on that, if I were you," the Human said. "However, that is not my thought."

The Commander moved forward, not willing to count on that.

Spock moved with her. "Have the grace to make your offer in front of us, James," he said in a sudden tone of vast weariness. "It concerns us."

The Human's eyes softened with compassion and with the look of being known too well. "Of course it does," he said softly, "but you do not have to hear it."

"You should not make it," Spock said, "but if you must, we must hear."

The Human nodded.

Omne grinned. "Ah, you are all so noble, and so vastly entertaining. I think I am going to enjoy this." He raised an eyebrow at the Human. "I trust you will make me your best offer."

"Certainly," the Human said. "It is not a question of nobility. It is a question of logic. Logic is the recognition of reality, even when it hurts, even when it conflicts with feelings, hopes. But reality also includes feelings, hopes, needs, purposes, rights. And—differences. Prices to be paid." He looked at Spock. "Jim Kirk offered to buy your freedom and mine. He has already—paid. Can—James—do less?"

"More," Spock said instantly. "Fight for both of you. Double or nothing. *He* would. He—*did*."

James Kirk spread his hands. "I am not he. There is—the difference. I have less to lose and nowhere to go. But I have—my price. And a stack of chips." He turned to Omne. "Their freedom. Spock's. Jim's. Hers. Full and complete. No strings. No scripts. Spock would see you in hell before he would do his script if you accept my offer. And probably even if you don't. And I buy only the real thing for Kirk—the life which should have been his. The *Enterprise*. Spock at his side. It will be easy enough to write a cover story for the death. It was an inpersonator who died. Plastic surgery. Unidentifiable charred remains. Regrettable error. Dastardly plot. The kidnapped Kirk was recovered by the astute Omne. Whatever."

"Your price seems a bit steep," Omne said, "especially since I have all four of you and have no need to let any of you go."

"You cannot, in fact, murder the Commander and Spock. It would reek to high heaven—and to the high command of Federation and Empire. You can be had, eventually. The same goes if you let either or both go—but in spades. Unless you have a hostage for both. You have just learned that Jim Kirk is not— necessarily—hostage for the Commander."

"But *you* are?" Omne said with amusement.

"I think so." The level eyes met hers.

She did not answer. But she had given her answer.

"And for Spock?" Omne asked.

"Yes."

Omne smiled. "You do not underestimate yourself. You may overestimate my interest in avoiding trouble. Is that your whole stack of chips?"

"No."

"What then, that I cannot have by keeping Jim Kirk—or both of you?"

The white shoulders leveled. "Ownership."

Omne laughed, startled. "*That* is your offer—the offer of the man who won't be owned?"

"Of that man." The shoulders and voice were steady. "That is why you have spoken of ownership, claimed it, wanted it—and wanted it only from a man who would not be owned."

"I own—the other."

"No. And you never will. You have taken what you wanted. You can never make him give it. Obedience. Acknowledgement. Consent. You have no threat left to make and no value to offer him."

"And you? Even if I accepted, would that not make you the man who can be owned?"

James Kirk shook his head. "In *that*, there is no dif-

ference. You would always know it. You would own
the unownable."

Omne smiled thinly. "I grant that it would be a de-
licious paradox. I grant, even, that no threat would
move you, either. But I do not think that I care to buy
you only with the value of other lives."

"*That* is the difference." The white shoulders
stretched. "You have also another value which you can
offer only to me. Yourself. You *are*—my creator. You
have created me—and my unique metaphysical problem. You are my Pygmalion, my Frankenstein. And I
am your own particular monster. It is a kind of bond.
I can stay here for a thousand years—or until we settle
with it."

Omne stood silent, and the Commander knew suddenly that he was buying it. James Kirk had found
Black Omne's price.

Omne gathered himself with the look of making one
more effort. "I could create another."

"He would not be me. He would not be the first.
Not the first ever to have to face the issue—and you.
If I stay, you will never create another. He would be
missing—too much. From the moment of creation,
there is—a difference. So—that also is a value, for me.
It ends with me—and you. A private universe here, for
two, and the universe goes on undisturbed."

"While we two settle with the problems of life and
death and immortality," Omne mused. "The solution
has a certain elegance, a certain grandeur. My compliments."

"Your acceptance will do. Do you call my—raise?"

"The original—against *my* original," Omne laughed.
"I could not have chosen either better. Both worth a
galaxy's ransom. Both with an understanding of—
elemental needs. Both with a gambler's nerve." The
black eyes narrowed. "But—you are both masters of
bluff. The price is steep, James, for both of us. I have
the chips to call. Do you? You've shoved an I. O. U.
into the pot. It requires—a down payment. An earnest
show of good faith. Of honor." Omne glanced at

Spock and the Commander. "And—it requires co-signers. Will they stand tied for it?"

James Kirk looked at Omne unflinchingly, then at Spock and the Commander. "I will—beg—them to, by their love, by my right—and the right of Jim Kirk. It is the only way." He grinned at them fractionally. "A crooked game—but the only game in town. You are not to worry. I have the chips."

She found that she could not even shake her head for watching. So this was how the man of command would—beg.

"Prove it," Omne said, his eyes on the man in white, his gun on the motionless Vulcan.

James Kirk stepped forward slowly, lightly, no limp in his walk, stressing ease, stressing ownership of the chips, stressing the wealth of the willingness to pay the price.

"I can afford the luxury," he said and sank to his knees in front of Omne.

Not a line of the kneeling body betrayed fear or horror. But she saw the fine hair standing in the frozen chill of gooseflesh on the back of the bowed neck.

"So can I," Omne said. And looked down.

She moved. But Spock was already a blur of motion. His boot caught the gun and sent it flying.

And in the same split moment he had lifted the Human and flung him into her arms.

She caught him as Spock took a stand before them to shield them with his body. "I am changing the name of the game," he said.

She saw Omne set to go through Spock that instant, then saw the black eyes calculate chances and speculate on what she would do with the stunned Human.

Omne straightened. "Name it," he said to Spock.

The Human gained his feet slowly in her arms, started to lunge forward, was held. "Let me go!" he gasped. "Spock, *no!*"

"New script," Spock said. "I will not have this double die."

"I wasn't going to die, Spock," the Human said, but his breath had caught in something very like a sob.

"It would have been death for you, and worse. I told you. You are not expendable."

"And—" the Human's voice caught—"your Kirk is?"

"You are both 'my' Kirk," Spock said.

"It is *his* life you are throwing away. Or worse that you are condemning him to," the Human answered.

"Possibly, James," Spock said. "It remains to be seen." He did not look back, but he seemed to see them. "Commander, will you take him away?"

She said instantly, "James. Come."

She quickly brought her arm up under the Human's thighs and carried him away and out, as Omne roared and lunged for Spock.

CHAPTER XV

Spock leaped aside with a slash of his bladed hand to Omne's shoulder, and a smash of a boot at a knee to bring the big man down.

Omne fell heavily, rolled up.

Spock twisted in air to land on his feet and saw the Commander carrying James.

Keep the trust, Spock thought, wishing that he could reach her mind to think it to her. Please be able to keep the trust.

He smashed a boot into Omne's kneecap and vaulted away.

He must adopt Kirk's tactics. The giant had all the advantages—the weight, the size, the fury.

Only Spock's fury matched the giant's—and *that* the Vulcan in him must master.

As an officer he had fought to kill, and killed when duty demanded. But he had never fought in the lust to kill, not even fully as a Vulcan when any Vulcan would have—in the arena of challenge, against Kirk.

But he was fighting in the lust to kill now. For Kirk. For both of him.

And for both of him Spock must not kill.

He couldn't risk it in a thousand years. He would never find Kirk. Never know whether the dead giant was alive and with Kirk. . . or coming after James. . .

The giant's bull charge swerved with deceptive speed, anticipating the direction of Spock's evasion. Massive hands smashed into the Vulcan's neck and low over his heart, and a knee caught him in the groin.

He rolled end over end and crawled to get away, fighting blind agony, scuttling around a corner as the giant dived, sparing no thought for dignity.

There is no pain, he told himself, clamping down with all of the Vulcan training and all his will. It was not enough, but it would have to do.

He gained his feet.

His calculator could estimate the giant's exact power now, and did so, unbidden, dispassionately reporting minute odds that Spock would leave the room alive, even if he fought to kill. And still more microscopic odds if he did not try to kill but tried to take the giant hulk apart until a forced mind-probe would rip out by the roots the knowledge of Kirk's location.

It was against the deepest custom of privacy. The forced probe was forbidden. But it could be done, and would.

And Spock knew that his calculator was right. But it was also wrong.

He would win.

He had to win.

He slugged a fist into Omne's stomach.

CHAPTER XVI

The Commander ducked in through the door with the Human, steadying him on his feet and stepping back to put her back against the door.

A quick sweep of his eyes determined that there was no other door in the small office, as she had remembered from their searches. Then his eyes met hers and said that he would go through her, one way or another.

When low, urgent words had not worked as she carried him out and down the corridor, he had tried plain effort. He could not quite bring himself to hit her, but he had arched and twisted and strained, skillfully, with all his muscle and quickness.

He could not believe hers.

And then he had hit her. A double chop to the shoulder nerves.

That was not to be taken lightly. He was powerful for a Human. But she had not let it loosen her grip.

But she had been holding him too tightly, hurting him too much. And if guards had stumbled across them. . .

"I cannot move you through the corridors like this," she said.

"No," he answered. "Commander, you *know* that we have to get back to Spock. It's not true. I won't throw my life away—and we can't let him do it. Please. It's *Spock*."

"It is—Spock—for me, too," she said heavily, feeling that fact pounding in every nerve. It was Spock—and he had no real chance at all without her. He was covering their retreat with his life, whatever he said, and their retreat was not possible unless this one yielded. Even if she knocked him out, not even her strength was equal to forty-odd floors of ladder tubes under his weight.

"I know it is Spock to you, too," he said softly. "Don't you see, we can't leave him. You can't take me and leave him. Double or nothing. He said it himself."

She nodded. "But he gave me—a trust."

But he said, "I'll be careful. My word on it."

Somewhere she found a smile. "I would take your word—for anything else."

He found the grace to grin, but his eyes crackled with anger and burned with desperation. "Damn it, I am not fragile. I'm a Starship Captain. I've fought the Gorn. I've fought Spock. I've fought Omne."

She nodded. "And you lost."

She saw him swallow, and knew that his body still burned with the memory of that loss.

"So, I lost," he said firmly. "There would be three of us now. But if I lost again, that would still be better than leaving Spock."

"Not for Spock. And not for me."

His brows furrowed, half following the thought, half dismissing the notion that he could mean more to her than Spock. He caught his lip between his teeth. "Then *you* go. Leave me. Lock me in if you don't trust me. But go to him now."

She reached out and put her hand on his shoulder, in silent token of how much that must have cost him. This one—first among men wherever he roamed—to let her do his fighting for him? There was depth beyond depth to this one. It might even give him some slim chance to survive when— "Not even that," she said, shaking her head regretfully. "Locks might not hold you—or might hold you too well. Guards could find you. Omne *would* find you if I lost with Spock. Spock would not forgive me. Nor I, myself. Spock has made his choice." She drew a deep breath and put her other hand lightly on his other shoulder. "And—I have made mine, James."

He took her face in his hands, promising the fullness of the kind of choice he could make, too. "Then—for *me*. Please."

He could melt stone, she thought, looking into the expressive face. Melt stone hearts. Vulcan. Romulan. The galaxy could not stand against him. How many hearts had he melted, how many faces warmed with those gentle, demanding hands? And yet she would have his innocence, this one who knew—and had never been touched. She would have him, if she let him have his way now. And if not, she could lose him forever. But she would lose him forever if she melted now.

"No," she said, not trusting herself to say more.

He backed away, disengaging his hands and hers. "Then listen. If you do not go, I will not move from this spot. If you carry me, you will never get me away. I guarantee I will fight you and slow you and try to break free, until we go for Spock—or Omne finds us. And when he does, I will renew my offer, for Kirk. You will never have me. But if you should, by some thousandth chance, get me away, you will still never have me if Spock dies. Unless you care to keep me as a captive."

"I would," she heard herself saying, and saw it jolt him. She lifted her chin. "I will. I am. Impasse, Captain." She threw back her shoulders in the stance of the Fleet Commander. "Two can play at that game."

His eyes suddenly believed her, and they were very close to tears, burning with rage and sheer frustration, one breath away from drowning in grief. "It is no game to me, and I am not playing."

"I know," she said. "Nor I."

He stood silent and she saw him struggling for thought against the impulse to take her by the throat. "Very well," he said in the voice of the Starship Captain. "What I said goes. But I don't play alpha games with lives, or—fight in a burning house. Someone

must always command. Command, Commander. Find
something useful to do, for both of us."

She found herself breaking into a smile. "You'll do,
James," she said, nodding. "I wonder if Jim could do
as well? Let's go."

He did not even say, "Where?" He followed her
through the door.

Kirk thrashed in nightmare, knew it was nightmare,
would not permit himself to dream it.

He twisted and rolled up, clawing his way to his
knees, two nightmares mingling. Omne— No, that was
the old nightmare. Reach for the new one, the quiet,
bitter one. The one with the knowledge that Spock was
dying at Omne's hands—

Kirk snapped his eyes open with a convulsion of his
whole body.

He was in the study. No, some other room. Darker.
There was some flicker of light. The surface under
him was a broad leather bench.

The second nightmare—where had it come from? It
seemed to be with him still, and he couldn't shake it.

He pried himself up and leaned his hands on his
thighs. A natural enough fear, he supposed. Spock
and Omne. Yet Spock could not be in here. But it had
seemed so vivid, not a fear but a fact. Leaden, in the
pit of his stomach. Burning in his scalded thighs and
raw hands.

What?

He snatched his hands up to examine them, put
them down to touch the insides of his thighs, the ach-
ing ankle—

No. That was not the pain of his own body. There
was no pain in his own body. Well, damn little, considering. And yet the pain was there. And the grief in
his mind. How—

Did it matter?

Spock—

He dragged himself off the bench, fighting unutter-
able weariness but calling on some last reserve. Get

moving. Find out. He saw that the flicker of light was from a bank of monitor screens. Good.

He tottered a little but did not sag—until his eyes froze on the two figures in black, locked in primordial combat. Omne and—dear God—Spock.

CHAPTER XVII

Spock kept moving.

They were both barely moving now, but he must not be caught by the bull rush or the bear hug. His broken ribs would not take it. Nor would the battered muscles, torn tendons, screaming nerves, gashed flesh. The Vulcan capacity against pain had long since been used and exceeded. He moved on nerve.

Omne's arms reached for him with the slowness of his own deadly weariness and pain. The black silk hung in rags and the bared arms, shoulders, stomach, were green with Spock's blood and blue-green with his own.

Omne was not merely a Vulcanoid, Spock thought again, slashing up at the reaching arms and throwing the giant off balance. He was of a related species, possibly. But he was in a class by himself. Spock knew that he had never met such a fighter in his life.

Omne swung back and Spock ducked, came up with his hands locked together and slashed at the bloody, heathen-idol face with great double-handed cleaver strokes.

He had to finish him.

Omne reeled, backpedaled, turned, and fled, staggering, lurching around the end of another lab bench.

Spock followed grimly, knowing that the giant had been looking for the fallen gun for some time. The search for the gun was a measure of the fact that Omne had never met such a man as the Vulcan, either, but Spock took small satisfaction in that.

He launched himself in a flat dive as he saw that this time the gun was there and Omne was going for it.

They fell and rolled, short of the gun. But Spock knew that this was final. He could not withstand the brute strength more than seconds.

And this time the knowledge drove his hands unerringly and unstoppably to the nerve pinch centers in both massive shoulders. He knew already that the centers were incredibly resistant, the nerves shielded by corded muscles like cabled steel. But the nerves were not invulnerable, and Spock's hands were durasteel forged in fire of purpose.

The giant's arms locked around Spock's broken ribs. Green haze blurred Spock's vision and blood pounded in his temples. But his hands were inexorable.

He saw white agony in the black eyes, and saw consciousness fading in them. He saw astonishment and black rebellion in the eyes which had never been defeated. Fear. But no surrender.

Creeping paralysis loosened the great muscles. The arms fell away and the corded abdomen went soft under Spock's. And still the black eyes did not yield the last shred of consciousness.

And—they *must* not, Spock realized suddenly. He needed the man's consciousness—as guide, as map to the labyrinth of mind, else Spock could grope forever in the darkness of inert memories for the one memory he needed.

Worse, he wanted the man to know what was happening, wanted him to feel the violation of his mind. And there was another memory which Spock wanted to rip out by the roots.

It was a thing no Vulcan could do, violating the deepest prohibition of a telepathic race—the forcing of a mind . . .

Spock loosened his hands. There was a time for breaking rules.

The black eyes cleared a little in the astonishment

of a new terror, as if Omne could read an intention worse than murder in Spock's face.

Spock locked his left hand again into the nerve center and unlocked his right to reach for the mind-hold on the battered face.

"What—" the puffed lips said almost silently, then more strongly, "—what are you going to do?"

Spock cracked blood loose from his own lips and knew that he had bared his teeth. "I am going to take him from you," he said, "all of him and both of him— the memory of him. I will find the memory and know it, all of it, and then I will take it away, bit by bit, and you will feel it going and know that it will be as if he had never been for you—never been seen, known, hurt—"

Omne's breath caught. "That is—worse than what I did."

"Yes," Spock said. "Would you care to beg?"

The lips twisted in a terrible grin. "Would it do me any good?"

"No," Spock answered, and he was certainly not smiling. "Would it have for *him*?"

Omne's laugh rumbled faintly in his throat. "No," he said, and the black eyes were unrepentant and unyielding, setting themselves to fight on the level of mind.

Spock went for the link, thrusting in with one single, tearing, unstoppable stroke and for one single objective: the one memory he had to know first before anything might stop him.

He found it by the very force of Omne's resistance, and then it was etched in Spock's brain: the route to Kirk, to Jim. And—the way out.

So much for business. Now for— Spock turned to reach for the other memory. And he met the shocking vitality of the dark mind, now past the first shock and mobilized against him.

It was another fight such as there had never been, and another one Spock would win because he had to.

He tore along the memory as on a trail of fire, letting it burn into his brain too fast for full comprehension. But it would be there later, and would never be erased. He let the great, dark mind batter at his own with savage, flailing blows, trying to reduce him to quivering pain with the sheer power of its black essence.

He knew that he would feel the pain, even absorb the essence, and not be reduced.

"Say good-by to it," he snarled aloud.

The black eyes locked with his in ultimate resistance.

And the great muscles heaved in convulsion. Pain hit Spock from directions he could not name—in body, in mind—but he held on.

The giant's great legs bucked and heaved his bulk backward, dragging Spock along.

Omne's hand reached the gun, and Spock's hands abandoned all else to lock on the thick wrist.

"Die, Vulcan," the black fury breathed.

The gun barrel shuddered by millimeters toward Spock's head, and he forced it away with all his strength, began to force it down towards Omne's head.

"*You* die," he said triumphantly and realized that he meant it. A thousand years of peace were cool in his mind, but the blood of millennia, of eons, pounded hot in his veins. And even the thousand years agreed: this one deserved it, for a crime worse than murder, for the hell he would unleash, for the lack of honor which made no peace possible. But it was simpler than that. For Jim. For James. Spock forced the gun down further. He had the vital knowledge. Let the man lose the memory in death. There was no other choice now, and he wanted none.

Take no chances.

He saw the real fear of death in Omne's eyes, now, and felt it in his mind. It was not a fear at the level of sanity. It stretched to the blackest deep levels of the great mind and the vast ego, the ultimate "I" which would not yield to dissolution.

Yes, that would be the worst fate for this one. Yes.

Spock jerked as if he had been hit and stopped the straining of his fingers for the trigger.

What if this one died—but the "I" did not dissolve? What if it disappeared into the hidden machinery of some hidden lab to rise from the ashes?

Spock called some last reserve of strength to hold against the gun with one hand and free the other to go for the neck pinch again.

"No," he said aloud and in the black mind. "'There will be no death to free you. Say good-bye.'"

Spock forced his mind to the root of the memory, began to pull— And the nerve hold was true. All of the giant's last strength was in the gun arm and was not enough to force it back to Spock. The paralysis was creeping over Omne.

Fear hit him—and the sudden knowledge that it was possible to fear worse than death. Then, slowly, the gambler's grin formed on the savage lips. "I—raise. Good-bye, Mr. Spock."

The man who hated death suddenly let the arm yield, let the Vulcan muscles force the gun down and up under Omne's jaw. Spock tried to recover to pull it away, but couldn't. "'Or—*au revoir*,'" the black mind said in the link.

Omne pulled the trigger.

Spock threw his mind back, fighting not to get caught in the death—true death, black and reaching. He felt the astonishment and rebellion of the great black mind, even in its choice . . .

Blackness reached for Spock, found him. He was not sure that he had lived through it. . .

CHAPTER XVIII

Kirk snapped himself out of it, berating himself for standing and watching, knowing that he could not have torn his eyes away.

But, damn it, he was letting himself get used to the idea that he was a prisoner, locked in, lost, unable to act.

To hell with that. He probably was locked in, but maybe not. And—not permanently. There was a way out of any box. This seemed to be only a monitor center. But there had to be a control center somewhere. A way out. Something he could use to get to Spock.

Just blunder his way out, maybe. He had seen how Omne released the baffle walls that blocked the passages of the inner labyrinth.

No. He had already seen that there were several exits. Which way?

His hands flew over the monitor controls, punching up new views. He wished that he had Spock's gift for reading alien machines. Or for calculating angles, correlating information. The Vulcan could probably back-figure from the multiple view angles to determine exactly where everybody and everything was— and draw a map.

Well, it was all done with the subconscious mind. Kirk tried to relax and let his operate.

He punched up several angles of the big lab where Spock had fought Omne—where both lay still as death. Don't think about that. He scanned the outer corridors. He found a place with three panels ripped off, one showing an entrance to the inner labyrinth. The screens offered miscellaneous angles of assorted inner labyrinth passages, branches, baffle walls.

And in a tiny corridor near one half-torn-down baffle wall, Kirk saw the Commander—and the other Kirk.

She was bending over the other Kirk, and he was half-sagging against the wall, his eyes withdrawn.

"James!" she said, shaking his shoulders gently.

The other—James, Kirk adopted immediately—tried to focus on the Commander. "It's Spock—" he said weakly. "Alive, I think, but so badly hurt. He couldn't keep me out at the last."

The Commander's hands were gentle on James's face, but her voice asked for a report. "And Omne?"

"Dead." James reported. "Killed himself."

She set her jaw. "Therefore—alive."

James's eyes widened. "Again— My God." He shook his head. "We have to go back, get to Spock."

"No. We have to get to Kirk. We don't know how long it will take Omne to live again. Spock's strength will serve him."

James swallowed. "Let me go to Spock."

She shook her head. "You're my guide to Jim. Are you still picking him up?"

"I—don't know. Can't feel anything but—Spock."

"Try." She took his shoulders again. "That's an order, James. Let's go."

James pried himself off the wall and turned with her. She ripped at the baffle wall.

Kirk shook himself. Damn.

On reflection, damn, and other words for when there were no words. And to hell with standing here.

He turned toward a door almost at random.

Let the subconscious do its stuff. Or whatever he had felt from James, whatever James felt from Spock. Whatever. Plain dumb luck. Whatever. Move.

As a matter of fact he did have some feeling that he could walk unerringly to Spock, like a somnambulist.

He tried not to think about the feeling or touch it. Let him walk in his sleep, but let him walk.

He pressed the catches to release the baffle walls and just moved.

Omne alive. Dear God, the "automatic machinery." But what a chance for Omne to take. Omne of all men.

And where was he—and how long would it take?

Would the next baffle wall reveal him standing, big as life, laughing?

Not yet, Kirk told himself firmly. Not yet.

He found himself in the study.

Good. The subconscious had its points. He scooped up the spray can from the couch.

He started to go through the door Omne had carried him through. Presumably he would find the Commander and James somewhere if they were on the right route.

Something seemed to draw him toward another door. He hesitated. It was only the vaguest of hunches. Probably a better chance with the passage he half-knew, and with the Commander.

But he turned to follow the hunch. He had bet on less before, and this one was calling him to Spock.

He passed an open closet and had some thought of clothes. But to hell with that, too. Later for that. He plunged in and broke into a lope.

Baffle walls and branches here, too, but he chose without hesitation, found the hidden studs to release the blocking panels. Still, he would have played hell even getting out without whatever was guiding him. Or without the secret of the control studs. Omne must have supposed that he wasn't in any condition to have noticed that.

Kirk came to a place where the maze widened into an alcove; then he burst through into the big lab, spotted the two still figures near the end of one aisle, and broke into a run.

He dropped down beside Spock, meaning to feel for a pulse, finding himself just kneeling to take the limp shoulders in his hands, press his face and ear against the back. Yes, the Vulcan heart was still beating, lower down, wrong place—

Hell, right place! Lovely, ridiculously fast beat.

"Spock!"

He rolled the Vulcan off Omne's body and into his own arms. Careful of broken bones, he told himself; but he wanted to carry the Vulcan away from the smell and sight of death, the blasted skull, the blood. And guards might be searching for the source of the shot.

Kirk rose carefully to his feet, cradling the living weight, heavier than a Human would have been, but seeming light to him now.

He found a low bench in the alcove inside the labyrinth entrance, nudged the panel closed with his shoulder, and decided against trying for the study. He knelt and settled his burden gently, extracting the spray can from the hand cradling the shoulders.

He started on the face. The soft spray seemed to foam up, absorbing blood, clearing it chemically, smoothing down to a skinlike film. But he had to ease cuts and splits together, almost remolding the face to its familiar shape.

That done, he could think about the body.

Internal injuries he could do nothing about. Spock's Vulcan healing would have to take care of that, until and unless they could get him to Sickbay. Kirk didn't know whether to hope that the Vulcan healing trance would set in fully, healing quickly, but keeping the Vulcan catatonic, requiring slaps to bring him out of it. They needed to move, if Spock could. But Kirk knew how the sickbay in the can eased pain as if it soaked in along the nerves. That, at least, he could do.

Spock's shirt was in shreds. Kirk tore it off, worked over the chest, felt broken ribs. Damn. If they hadn't punctured lungs, or worse. . . Kirk didn't try to turn or lift him to work on the back, but filled his hands with spray foam and slipped them under to spread it. Then the arms and the battered hands.

The jeans were heavier, and they and the gunbelt might have protected the lower body a little. He unfastened both, thinking how Spock would raise an eyebrow—or possibly hell.

"Uniform of the day, Mr. Spock," Kirk murmured, deciding that it was just as well that the Vulcan couldn't hear—or see his friend's face. The bruises— Kirk thought even that the tip of a hipbone was shattered. How had the Vulcan lived, or moved?

Kirk did what was needed. He was well down the thighs, starting on shattered kneecaps, with the jeans slipped down around the boots, when Spock said, "That will be enough, Captain."

Kirk whirled, caught the shoulders, didn't try to still his laugh or stop the tears that threatened to spill. "Spock!" He let a long, slow grin develop, thought that a tear or two did spill—his choice, now—finally added, "You old horse thief."

"Why should I abduct such an equine, Captain?" Spock said in the manner of the old jokes, and Kirk knew that he had never been so glad to play straight man to a Vulcan.

"Well, we might even use one to ride out of this horse opera," he said, and then put a hand on Spock's face. "Welcome back, Mr. Spock."

"Yes—" The pause was very long and the Vulcan eyes searched his face, seemed to drink it in, reached long fingers to brush dampness from his cheeks. "—Jim." The voice was utter satisfaction, undisguised and uncovered, the face calm, but not wearing its mask.

Kirk bowed his head in acknowledgement. "Spock," he answered in the same voice.

But he thought that perhaps neither one of them could hold the moment much longer, nor did they need to. "Now, about those knees—"

Spock raised his head, a shoulder, tried to sit up. "I am functional—"

"Lie still, Mr. Spock!" Kirk touched the shoulder back down, and Spock resisted for an instant, then settled back as if obedience were a luxury.

"Yes, Captain."

Kirk grinned and turned and finished with the knees, went to the boot line, while Spock stared rather fixedly at some point on the ceiling.

"That really is enough, Jim. The internal healing is also sufficiently under way. In a few moments I shall be able to move—and we must."

"You'll stay right here for a few minutes, at least," Kirk said. "I think it might take Omne as much as an hour, maybe more. It did with—James."

Spock raised an eyebrow. "You seem remarkably well informed. I am also at something of a loss to know how you found me. That was supposed to be my act."

Kirk grinned. "I steal all the best lines." He sobered. "Viewscreens. I saw the last of the fight. Tried to figure the angles. But I don't know. Something funny going on with James, me, you. Maybe that led me."

Spock sighed. "Possibly." He met Kirk's eyes. "I am—linked to James."

Kirk felt his jaw harden a trifle, but he nodded. "I know."

"It is directional," Spock said, "but I could not reach you. He could. And I, through him."

"It's—all right, Spock. Later for that."

"You do not understand," Spock said. "We were—with you—feeling with you—until you lost—the pain."

"With me—?" Kirk said and felt himself sinking down to sit on his heels. "Dear God." Spock's hand found his shoulder. Finally he lifted his eyes to meet the Vulcan's. "I'm sorry, Spock. Hell for you."

"For you."

Kirk found a small smile somewhere. "All right. But I am all right."

He straightened his shoulders and reached a hand to Spock. "I think we had better go mind the store, if you're ready."

The Vulcan took the hand. "Ready, Captain."

Kirk steadied the Vulcan on his feet, tried to offer support and draw an arm around his shoulders. But the Vulcan gained balance and indicated firmly that he was all right.

He looked Kirk over critically. "It is I who should be going over you," he said.

Kirk laughed. "Hell, I thought you knew. Omne fixed me up." His hands indicated the state of his undress.

Spock flickered an eyebrow. "Uniform of the day, Captain." He frowned. "However, the spray conceals even more pain than it heals. You could have serious injuries still. Human bones. I can hardly credit that you survived Omne."

Kirk smiled bitterly. "He was going easy on me, obviously. Anyway, I'm not hurting, Spock. Not to speak of."

"It is not speaking of it which worries me," Spock said.

Kirk grinned. Back to normal. "Well, come to think of it, I *am* hurting, some, but it's not—me." He scooped up the spray can. "Can you contact James? Tell the Commander to stop tearing up the walls. We'll get to them. They were—coming for me."

"They know. I could not keep my improvement from James. They have reached the study."

"Have them wait," Kirk said. "Let's go." He led the way into the labyrinth tunnel, through the baffles he had left open, closed another one behind them. After a while he looked back to grin. "And let's hope that I can carry off the September Morn act as well as—James."

The Commander was standing with her hand on James's shoulder, with the air of having, firmly, made him sit down on the couch.

James flashed a tiny, quick look to Kirk acknowledging that fact—and a kind of astonished wonder at it.

But his eyes were for Spock and so were the Commander's. They were drinking in the Vulcan, the living sight of him, and Kirk did not blame them.

Kirk handed the spray can to James. "Try this on

your hands and legs. It looks like we're in this together."

James's grin answered his. "Sorry, Captain. I'll see what I can do. Thank you, Jim."

So it was to be as simple as that—name and rank. "*My* thanks, James," Kirk said. "For everything." He looked up to meet the woman's eyes. "And—to you also, Commander."

"My pleasure, Captain," she said gravely, just a faint crinkle around her eyes acknowledging his nakedness and her appreciation. And then she did smile. "The original—to the life."

He laughed softly. "*I* should have a word or two to say about *that*." He bowed fractionally. "It would have been—my pleasure."

She smiled a little archly. "Come now, Captain, you wouldn't want to spoil the value of a good secret. Would you defend a lady's honor by calling her a liar?"

"I'd call her—skillful at bluff."

She laughed silently. "Oh, well, precious few secrets around here today." She turned to James. "And time for still fewer. Give me that can and join the Captain."

"*What*—?" James said as she appropriated the can.

"Well, it will hardly work through clothing," she said. "As the Captain found out. Even, I'll warrant, Mr. Spock. What makes you different?"

James contrived to look indignant. "Well, for openers, I don't have much clothing in the first place. Most of me is pretty—accessible. Give me the can and I'll—"

"One does not slide down a pole only on—the accessible." She tweaked the opening of the tunic aside, revealing less severe friction burns on the chest, abdomen, disappearing down into the briefs.

Abruptly Kirk became aware of all of that, too. Damn.

"In the second place," James said, coloring, "the agreement about—command—was only for the duration."

"The duration endures," she said. "I trust it will endure for a long time. Come now, you have no secrets from me. Let's go."

Kirk looked at them speculatively as their eyes locked in silent contest.

And Spock suddenly appeared from somewhere and dropped a robe around Kirk's shoulders, dropped another into James's lap.

It broke up the contest and the two looked up in astonishment.

Kirk slipped into the robe—and practically disappeared into it. It looked like Omne—something in black and softness, a sensuous velvet.

Kirk slashed the tie tight around his waist and found Spock turning up six inches of sleeve for him and looking at him oddly.

Kirk shrugged. "The bigger they come—" He gentled his voice. "I didn't break into little pieces, Spock. Thank you."

"Captain," Spock said grimly. "I was in his mind—at the last. You have no idea. The malevolent intention. For you, for James. For the galaxy. And—the scope of the mind, the size. And he still lives—in the same galaxy with the two of you." Spock looked down, somehow managing to stress Kirk's smallness even against himself.

"All right, Spock," Kirk said with more calm than he felt. "And—on the same planet. We'll get moving. And it may have to be the hard way. All I found was a monitor screen room." He looked down at James. "I suggest—one way or another—within the next couple of minutes."

James grinned wryly and nodded.

Kirk drew Spock aside with the manner of a briefing and turned both their backs on the other two. He could hear little noises in the background. And he could feel—well, damn near feel—slender, strong hands—

"You might," he said firmly to Spock, "be able to

coax those screens to find us a control room, even a transporter room."

"Not necessary, Captain," Spock said. "When I was looking for the way to you, I also found the way out. The control room. Very near to where you were. I can find it."

Kirk remembered not to pound him on the back, put it into a grin. "And Omne's lab?"

"No, that I did not get, even at the last. He guarded it. Do you know, he never believed I could beat him? Couldn't believe that I *had*. Wouldn't give up—purposes—elemental needs. Wouldn't believe that he could die—even knowing that he would live again. Didn't believe it even as he died—"

Spock reeled against him, and Kirk caught his shoulders and held him until the moment passed.

"You almost liked him, didn't you?" Kirk said.

"No," Spock said. "But I *saw* him."

Kirk nodded. "I did, too, a little."

"And did not forgive."

"No."

"Nor I."

"We're talking about him as if he *were* dead."

Spock nodded. "He *is*. We have to kill him."

Kirk kept his back to the bed, but permitted himself to check on the progress of James and the Commander—at least permitted his attention to shift to it; he really couldn't help being aware.

The two weren't really embarrassed with each other, he realized. The touch was medical, but not impersonal, and not resented. As if a bond had formed very quickly and included even the fact of her strength.

Well, he was capable of that, Kirk thought. Why not James? But it was a little disconcerting to feel the same kind of half-playful, half-serious challenge he would have put up. And her silent, laughing, teasing response—

Kirk drew Spock a couple of steps further from the

bed, but it didn't seem to help. "This—between James and me," he asked quietly. "What is it? It seems to be getting stronger. It's not—through you?"

"No," Spock said. "Nature unknown, Captain. I hypothesize a kind of resonance. The too-similar structure, similar minds. Possibly fading with different experience, renewing itself again with closeness or increased knowledge. Disturbing for you. Possibly dangerous."

Kirk grinned faintly. "Disturbing, at least. Dangerous?"

"If it persisted, you would always be too aware of each other. Feeling each other's pain, other sensations. Distracting. In a fight, possibly deadly."

"I see what you mean," Kirk said. "Well, later for that, too."

He felt that the clothes situation was practically in hand, and after a moment turned. James was just pulling the robe tight and the thin silk showed that he had repossessed the briefs. Kirk rather envied him that, but not the flamboyant silk of his robe. He supposed that it was a fair contest for who looked or felt most ridiculous. The Commander finished with the sleeves and Kirk said, "Let's go. Lead on, Mr. Spock."

Spock nodded and led through the tunnel to the viewscreen room. Kirk followed, then took the lead to press the studs as Spock picked another tunnel, guided Kirk with a touch on his shoulder.

They broke through presently into a large control center, and Kirk followed Spock to what looked like the main console. Spock scanned the controls and translated quickly. "A transporter. Override controls for most systems. Everything we should need—except that I do not expect Omne's secret lab to show on any map, plot, or viewscreen." He turned to face Kirk. "However, we have control of the main planetary defense shields."

"Then we must beam to the ships," the Commander said immediately, "and destroy the planet."

"Planet?" Kirk said, feeling a little slow.

"No option," the Commander said. "Omne—and Omne's process—must not be loosed on the galaxy, nor on the two of you. It really will buy the galaxy, and he knows how to use it. Empire, Federation, your species and mine, Klingons—any species capable of personal loyalties and loves. Perhaps even others. Altered duplicates, impostors, one mind in another body. The evil is unlimited—and only we can limit it."

"Find Omne," Kirk said. "*He* is the evil."

"Not possible," the Commander said, meeting his eyes. "While we looked, he could be moving, blocking our escape, working from an auxiliary control system. He could be anywhere within thousands of miles. It would fit his psychology. No half-measures, and we can take none. No, Captain, the planet has to go."

"There are innocent lives here, too," Kirk said.

She nodded. "I am not without feeling for them, Captain. But I am a soldier. There are innocent lives in any war. These, at least, made the choice of an outlaw planet. And they are a few thousand. But this is, in any case, war—the most important ever fought in the galaxy. One blow now—or a long, terrible agony." She drew herself up very tall and did not flinch from his eyes. "If you cannot do it," she said simply, "I will."

"If I want it done," Kirk said, "I will do it."

"Captain," Spock said. "There is no question of the Prime Directive here. It is an artifical culture, an assembly of legends and license, outcasts and outlaws. And—those here have—chosen. There are others who have not—in their billions and hundreds of billions. I do not say that we have the right, but it is possible that we have the duty."

Kirk turned to him slowly. "It is you who are my—balance, sometimes my conscience. Do you say war, Spock?"

"I say there can be a time when there is no way to choose the right, because there is no right left to choose." He looked down steadily at Kirk. "It is why one makes rules not to be broken, and chooses a man able to break them." His eyebrow bowed in what was almost a smile. "I have never needed to be your conscience, but I suspect that this is your time to be mine. I think I know your choice—and how long we may live to regret it."

Kirk had to smile. He nodded. "Possibly for the next thousand years." He turned to the Commander and shook his head. "For once it is I who have to plead the Prime Directive, or perhaps even an older rule than that. I can't murder the innocent to get to the guilty. I can't count numbers. The right of a single innocent life has to stand against the 'greater good' of billions—or we have made no gain in the last thousand years, and won't in the next."

The Commander raised an eyebrow in admiration, but there was something in her eyes which was still more solid. "So this is the man half a galaxy damns for trampling 'rights' and taking morality into his own hands?" She shook her head. "I admire your conscience, Captain, and Mr. Spock's. I will take this upon my own. I will transport to my ship. What I do will not be your responsibility."

"It will be, if I don't stop you," Kirk said.

"How would you propose to stop me?" she said mildly.

He had a small feeling that his mouth was hanging open. "I thought we were in this together," he said. "But as far as that goes, there's the equipment—" He gestured to Spock.

"I can handle the equipment," she said.

Slow, he thought. Hadn't really occurred to him. But why not? His eyebrows conceded the point. Well, then, cut through to the essence. "I suppose, if it comes to that, there are three of us."

She arched an eyebrow. "Are there? Are you sure? You see, it does sometimes come down to numbers. But—if there are, Mr. Spock is badly injured and the two of you are only Human."

"You wouldn't—" Kirk began.

"Wouldn't I?" she said. "To leave all three of you

free of the guilt of this? I know that I am able to bear
it. I don't know that about you, or James. Mr. Spock
could, but I doubt that he would bear your condemnation, Captain."

"I suppose you don't have to worry about my condemnation." Kirk said evenly. "But what about
Spock's? What about—James's?"

"James has not spoken. You have assumed that you
have the right to decide. Possibly he has, too. By what
right? He is not under your command. He was
pledged to be under mine. How is your honor on that
point, James?"

James shook his head. "My honor is not pledged to
accept your command about *this*. I don't play games
with lives. If I have assumed anything about rights, it
is that someone must command, and we don't fight
under Omne's gun. However, I agree with Jim. I
would not, in any case, let you take this on yourself. If
we must fight you, we must, and you will have to go
through me to get to them."

She nodded. "That can be arranged."

"And—you don't have to worry about my condemnation?" James asked.

She lifted her head. "I am prepared to worry."

Spock finished some setting and turned to her.
"And—mine?"

"Your condemnation, among other things, I would
like to avoid, Mr. Spock. The other two I could deal
with without undue damage to myself or them. Pack
them off to my ship and resume discussions under
more propitious circumstances, after the fact. You, in
your present condition, I might very possibly kill, and
it is conceivable that you could still kill me, and
would have to. That is illogical, Mr. Spock. Wasteful."

Spock bowed an eyebrow. "It is all of that."

"The logic is that it should not be Jim's decision, or
James's. They are being noble about it. I told you how
tired I am of nobility. It is lovely, but it has cost us a
great deal before, and this price is too high. A single
innocent life? Yes! Two. *Theirs*. And—more than life.

The worst threat is to *them*. Men have faced death before and will again. But they are the first to face *this*. You know better than any man Omne's intention—and his power."

"I do," Spock said.

"Do you? And have you turned your imagination loose on it? He will be after them. He will make another copy, but he will still want these. The original, and his particular first creation. The experiences they have had today. The great adversary relationship. The contest with Jim. The offer James made—would have to make again on threat to you. The contest with you—knowing what each and both mean to you. Even, with me. You can try to protect and defend them. How will you defend both? How would they defend you, if you were captured—except with—offers?"

"Stop it!" Kirk said, seeing Spock's face. "Whatever this leaves us with, we just have to live with it. We don't have to dwell on it."

"We do," she said. "We have to tell ourselves exactly what we face. We will fight Omne—I too, whatever you do. And we can lose. We *will* lose things we may not be able to stand, if we do not cut this at the root." She turned to Spock again. "Either one of them or both, to death or a thousand years, uncounted thousands of years, of—slavery. Omne can prepare another retreat where we can never find him. Probably has one already. Several. Needing only to get out to get to them. He will fight us across the galaxy—*for* the galaxy—take it over, if for no other reason than to defeat us. He will try to set us at each other's throats, Federation against Empire, a war of all against all, for his vengeance—because we beat him, and he will not be beaten. We made him die—and of all men he would not die."

"That is true," Spock said, his eyes looking into some darkness.

"It is not all," she said inexorably. "He will do the same to others, wherever he finds love. Of all men, he hates love—and wants it. But he will begin and end with us. We showed him what love meant. Jim? James? There will be James II, James III. Omne will make copies. Some to keep. Some to—sell. We will see Kirks sold by Orion slave traders—along with green dancing girls. And each one will *be* Jim and James. Each as brave, as real, as valuable. Are we to spend our lives rescuing Kirks—and if we do, what will we do with them—or they with themselves?"

"Dangerous for him," Kirk said, knowing that he had to stop her somehow. Try logic. "Copies to keep, possibly. The other would reveal his process. Have everybody in the galaxy hunting him."

"Yes," she said, "and would he care—when he can go to ground as thoroughly as this on a single planet? When he cannot die? And—it does not help us. If the mere existence of the process becomes known, others will invent it. A question of time. Not much time. Then every miscellaneous dictator in the galaxy will have it. My Empire. Do you trust even your Federation? What about Klingons? Who is to be trusted with immortality as a weapon? Would you trust yourself not to sell your soul for a recreation of Spock on some day when he is killed?"

Kirk took a deep breath. "No," he said.

"Nor I," she said, answering him but looking at Spock. "And—why should he *not* live again? If it is possible—why should he not? Why should you not? Men of great value, to themselves and others. Women. T'Pau of Vulcan will die soon. Why not she? Why not Ambassador Sarek? Why not Spock's mother, Amanda? Why not your mother, Jim? Or mine? But then—why not anyone's mother, father, child, love? Why not the unloved? But it is bound to be an expensive process. Who pays? And who decides who is to live again?"

"I grant the difficulty," Kirk said, "even—the impossibility. But men have faced some such problems, on a smaller scale, with many medical advances."

"And never fully solved them," she said. "But this *is* a final solution. And the fight over it could be the war to end the world—to end civilized, stargoing life in the galaxy. To reduce planets to rubble—or stack them fourteen deep in people."

Kirk sighed and nodded. "I know. Of course, I know. But that kind of problem has been faced before, too, and sometimes the only solution is to fight it through and come out the other side—even if it means that you have to claw your way up out of the rubble again. What you see is true. What you don't see is that Pandora's box can't be closed again. The Pandora's box of technology never can. The atomic bomb couldn't be uninvented. If one country hadn't invented it, hadn't used it, another would. There is a state of the art in these things. Think of all the simultaneous discoveries just on Earth, on your planet. If we destroyed this planet today, somebody would have the process within years, at most decades. No, I say that we cannot buy that at the price of lives—or why can we not buy it at the cost of one planet after another? And what would that make us? No. But there has been Hope in every Pandora's box—and it's been enough. It will have to be enough for us. We'll fight, but it will have to be the right fight."

She shook her head. "I agree—but I cannot agree. The process does not have to be in the hands of Black Omne. Nor loosed just yet. If I were Pandora, I would have clamped the lid back down—and blown up the castle. And I will. I'll buy those years or decades. I can afford the luxury." She turned to Spock. "And you, Spock? It is not only immortality. It is a personal contest, where we—and ours—stand to lose the most. Think of Omne's black-devil imagination. Think of another mind in Kirk's body, rung in on you on any day. Omne's mind, even. You or I might detect it with the link. But think of the opposite. Omne will have body scans of you and me. We went through his transporter. Do you care for the thought of Jim or James up against Omne in the body of Spock?"

"No," Spock said hollowly.

"And will you stand for it? I will not. And I will do this for you, too. But I do not wish to have to go through you. Nor him, them. Choose now. Does he command you in this?"

Spock looked down into her face, and Kirk saw that the Vulcan looked into the pits of hell. The fire of their ancient, savage ancestry was in both faces, and Kirk knew suddenly that he did not command Spock in this. Never had. Never would. There was a point where strength ruled and elemental needs commanded.

And the Vulcan was the power in this room.

"No," Spock said, "but you will have to go through him to get out, and through me to get to him. Both of him."

She stood as if she would, and Kirk set himself to dive before she could get to those broken ribs, saw from the corner of his eye James doing the same.

But she looked only at Spock.

"That was what I wanted to know," she said, and stepped back a fraction. "You keep a trust, too, Mr. Spock. And I—" She lifted her head. "Even if I could go through that—I would not."

"Bluff?" Spock asked.

"Called," she said.

Spock nodded. "A no-limit game." He turned to Kirk. "I suggest that we depart."

Kirk settled his shoulders. "When you're ready, Spock," he said, not even testing the tenuous fiction of command.

But Spock said, "Ready now, Captain. I have taken the liberty of setting a destruct in the shield circuits. It will take some time to repair and give us some. I do not entirely reject the Commander's logic. Or yours. But I recommend we adjourn to the *Enterprise*. I have set the transporter for McCoy's office and for the four of us."

Kirk nodded. "Thank you, Mr. Spock." He turned to the Commander. "We will need—your word."

She arched an eyebrow. "My parole as a prisoner?"

"Only if that is necessary," Kirk said. "But I will not have you challenge Spock again."

"Or you?" she asked.

"Or me on my ship."

"I would not respect less, Captain," she said. "And I perceive that it *is* your ship, in spite of all. That, also, I wanted to know."

"Mr. Spock has just said that I do not command him," Kirk said with great clarity.

"And proved that you command him more than you ever knew."

That, too, Kirk thought. Of course, that, too. "Do I have your word, Commander?" he said heavily.

"For the duration, Captain."

The duration—endures, he thought. God, forever. It was catching up with him. He waved her and James toward what passed for transporter positions here and followed silently, feeling his legs go suddenly heavy. He started to pause behind Spock at the console, couldn't think of anything to say. It had been in his defense, after all. He put his hand on the Vulcan's shoulder in some kind of acceptance, apology, comfort—something.

And the Vulcan's eyes said about the same, said—hell of a universe.

Kirk smiled thinly and made it to the transporter platform, saw Spock set a delay and come to join them.

Bones, Kirk thought. No, no way not to spring this on him if he was there. Spock would have known they would need the privacy of his office, and Sickbay, and Bones.

Spock seemed to read the thought. "It is the kind of shock one can take," he said in the tone of a confession.

Kirk grinned and felt a little better, saw sparks start to spill from the console as Omne's transporter effect took them. It was silent, he realized.

CHAPTER XIX

McCoy thought that he would raise his head from the desk in just a moment, just another minute, maybe.

Get on the horn and check with Scotty for the umpteenth time. Any word from Spock? Any progress on breaking through on the lock on the transporter, penetrating the damn shields? But he already knew what the answers would be. Same answers, hour after hour.

He had tried drinking and given it up when he stayed altogether too sober. And Scotty, of course, had not even tried and was even soberer, feeling the weight of command settle on his shoulders, beginning to fear that it might stay there this time.

Yes, have to do something for Scotty, even if it was only the umpteenth question for the umpteenth time. In just a second—

"Bones—"

The soft voice— God damn it, he was *not* going to start hallucinating!

The hand touched his shoulder and he flung himself to his feet, stumbling.

Jim caught him.

He couldn't speak. He pried himself away to look. Not possible! But the face—could not be another face like that in the universe. The eyes. The body under his hands, in his arms. No android body, surely, no illusion— Oh, God, it could be any of those things, but somehow he knew that it wasn't.

"Jim! Oh God, Jim—"

"It's true, Bones. It's all right now. It's me."

Stop blubbering, McCoy told himself. You're a doctor, not a—

He couldn't think of anything. He lifted his head and started to seize the broad shoulders, swing him around, look at him—

And met resistance. "A moment, before you turn," Kirk said. It was an order and McCoy blinked and stood quiet, trying to come to attention and reorganize his mind.

"Spock?" he asked.

"He's all right," Kirk said. "I am, too. However, there are two of me. It's complicated, but that's all right, too. Also, we have a guest, and—she's all right. Sorry to spring it on you, but we'll explain."

The arms let him turn—caught him when he sank down on the desk, not sure whether he was feigning the sagging of his knees.

"I don't think I want to know," he said in his best manner of long-suffering.

Spock raised an eyebrow. "Would you call that an emotional display to end all emotional displays, Doctor?"

"In a pig's eye," McCoy murmured happily.

Kirk caught Spock's nod. "Captain, Mr. Scott."

"Of course." Kirk settled his shoulders and nodded toward the intercom. "Tell him to sit tight. We'll—"

But the intercom burst into life, together with alert signals. "Intruder alert," Scott's voice said, "intruder alert. Planet shields down. Trace of planet transporter signal indicates target within this ship. Security, institute Class Two search. All personnel, yellow alert. Scott out."

Spock traded glances with Kirk, and Kirk waved him to the intercom. "Spock here," the Vulcan said. "Cancel intruder alert, Mr. Scott. I am responsible."

"Spock! Where in the name—? Yes, sir. You're aboard? Hell's breakin' loose. Gabble of communications. Planet says Omne's been murdered, guards shot up. Romulan ships in an uproar. Their Commander is

overdue. Sub-Commander S'Tal's makin' noises like we
might have somethin' to do with it. Told me to produce her or else. Planet's looking for her, says she
shot up guards, maybe Omne. One report says she
was seen with—Captain Kirk. Hysterical down there.
Stark ravin'." Scott sighed audibly. "Welcome aboard,
Mr. Spock."

"Thank you, Mr. Scott," Spock said. "On my way—"
Kirk put a hand on his arm. "Scotty," he said into
the intercom. "Tell the crew I'm alive."

"Captain! Jim? Jim!" Deep breath. "Aye, sir."

"That's the spirit, Scotty. Tell 'em I'll take—
complaints—later."

"Aye, sir. I'll tell 'em—what suits me." Sudden break
in the grinning voice. "Queen to King's Level Four,
Captain."

Kirk glanced at James, thinking how well that code
had served them before, how little it would serve them
against this. "Knight takes Queen, Mate," Kirk answered.

"Aye," Scott said with satisfaction.

"Hold the fort, Scotty. Five minutes. On my way.
Kirk out." He turned to the others, tuning Scott's voice
out in the background, and nearly bumped into
McCoy, who had repossessed his wits and his medical
scanner, had been running it over his back.

"You're not going anywhere," McCoy said flatly.

"Later, Bones. Prescribe some clothes out of your
famous medical stores. Then see to Spock." He saw
protests rising from McCoy and the Vulcan. "Don't
argue," he said in a voice that didn't permit it. McCoy
considered it anyway, shook his head, finally headed
for the cabinet where he rather sheepishly kept
clothes for Kirk and Spock in his private office, always complaining that he couldn't keep Kirk in shirts.

"Commander, a script," Kirk said, shifting his attention to her, thinking as he went. "I was kidnapped by
Omne and company. You rescued me. The Empire is
not bought with cheap tricks. Truce between honora-
ble enemies against cowardly deception and effort to

make you prisoner, too. Self-defense. Mr. Spock also discovered plot, challenged Omne to single combat by customs of this planet. Omne committed suicide when beaten. Now we could both shoot up the joint in retaliation and to stamp out future conspiracies, but we won't. Virtues of Empire and Federation. We'll ram the Prime Directive down their throats. No objection if they want to set up shop here as a refuge, but peaceful purposes only, or we'll quarantine and cut off trade. Joint announcement, you and me. We'll quibble over who gets the best lines. How about it?"

"Script?" she said with a slow smile. "It is the simple truth."

"That's the best kind," he grinned.

"It is not, however, the complex truth," Spock said. "There is still Omne. It leaves him armed and dangerous, his organization set up to function as a trust on death or disappearance. Perhaps we should require evacuation, at least dismantling of weapons and shields."

McCoy put a pair of pants in Kirk's hands and Kirk bent to pull them on under the robe. "That's never been very effective," he said, "and we'd have to shoot 'em up to some extent to do it. They have a right to defend what they've built here. A lot of it is of value. Research. Trade. Refuge—political criminals, even other criminals, perhaps. Remember Australia. No. But we may drive Omne out of this nest. I have a feeling that he was a loner in most of his evil purposes. Hard for him to function if he's dead. And hard to show up alive without revealing his process. Whereas we can't do a foot-by-foot search, even if they'd let us, for the same reason."

McCoy handed him a shirt and took the robe, and he felt the doctor's hand tracing the injuries under the spray film as he pulled the shirt over his head.

"Jim—"

Kirk turned to answer the pain in the eyes. "It's all right, Bones. I was—fixed—by an expert. Enough painkiller to hold a horse. It'll hold me till there's time for the real expert."

"News for you, Jim. Any painkiller you had is wearing off fast."

Kirk's eyes admitted to McCoy that it was not news, but hid it from the Vulcan. "Not bad yet," he said firmly and turned back. "Commander, you and I had better get going before your 'Tal develops a nervous trigger finger."

"He has been known to be impetuous," she said and moved toward the door.

Spock started for it, too. Kirk stopped him with a look. "You're out of uniform, Mr. Spock."

The Vulcan raised an eyebrow. "I hardly think that matters. However, I might point out that so are you." He looked pointedly at Kirk's bare feet.

"Well—I'll keep 'em off the viewscreen," he grinned. "No, Spock," he said firmly. "Sickbay for you. You're to let McCoy do his stuff, and do your Vulcan act. We still have problems to settle after we call off the war." He looked at James. "Will you see that he does it? And I'm afraid I'll have to ask you to explain to the Doctor, too."

"I'll take care of it," James said. "And—stay out of sight."

Kirk nodded to him soberly. "Thank you." He met Spock's eyes, saw reluctant acceptance, turned to the door. "Commander?"

She let him guide her through the door.

CHAPTER XX

Spock sat up.

James slapped his face.

"Again," Spock commanded, "harder."

James set his jaw and put muscle into it. Again.
Again.

Spock caught his wrist, remembering to be gentle.
"Enough. Thank you. I am revived."

McCoy swept the scanner over him. "But not recovered. "You didn't stay under long enough, Spock.
Those ribs and knees and hands are just beginning to
knit. And the internal injuries—I hate to complain
about a miracle. Anybody else'd be dead, but—"

"No miracle is involved, Doctor. Merely a useful
technique. It will be sufficient. The process will con-
tinue at a slower rate."

"Pain reading is still high enough to kill anybody."

"I am functional, Doctor, and I have functions to
perform. You will start on James now, and you will
also run the standard identity checks."

McCoy's eyebrows shot up. "I thought his identity
was not in question. He said you linked—"

"His identity is not," Spock said. "Whether we can
conceal or disguise it *is*."

"I don't follow you," McCoy said.

Spock looked at James, then back to the Doctor.
"The *Enterprise* cannot have two captains. But perhaps surgical alterations, special entry to Star Fleet
with another background, or a political position—
special ambassador—"

"Never work, Spock—records on every molecule of him, voice prints—"

"That should do it," Kirk said. "Take the con, firmed. James?"

James nodded. "Needs to be established. Might also give us a clue to the process. Doctor?"

"You're not in much shape for a check. I can't find the injuries, but you're hurting as bad as Jim."

"It will pass," James said quietly. "Let's go. Spock, you rest."

Spock sighed and lay back down in the manner of being put upon. Two of them!

"That should do it," Kirk said. "Take the con, Scotty. Commander?"

He led her quickly off the bridge, flashing looks to the bridge crew, again acknowledging their response to his return. Uhura had worked steadily, with tears drying on her cheeks.

But he couldn't take time for more. The turbo-lift doors closed and he said, "Sickbay." And the Commander caught him as he sagged.

She held him up, then bent quickly and picked him up.

"Put me down," he gasped, and considered himself lucky not to yell.

"Don't be silly," she said. "I can carry you easily."

"Damn it, not through the corridors of the *Enterprise!*"

She arched an eyebrow. "I daresay you've been carried to Sickbay before. You mean—not by a woman."

"Probably," he admitted. "What if I do? It's a tough idea to get used to. I don't mind if you have muscle—but do you have to throw your weight around?"

She shrugged as if his weight were not a problem. "Do you? It's a fundamental principle: if you've got it, you've got to use it."

A point, he thought with a weary effort at fairness. Didn't he use any muscle he had—and damn glad to have it? Enjoying it? If the shoe were on the other foot—? He let a rueful grimace concede the point. "Then—just put me down because—I'm asking. Would you have me carry you through your ship if you could walk—or crawl?"

She lifted her eyebrows, and her slow smile conceded a point too. "You'll do, Captain," she said and slowly swung him down.

He might have to crawl at that. He fought his knees while she kept her arm around him, and there was no teasing in her support now. "It's all right," she said softly. "You have every right. Don't fight it quite so hard. Surely you can accept a shoulder?"

He smiled weakly and put his arm around her, leaned on her heavily. Hard to believe such slimness could contain such strength. "Friends?" he whispered.

"Friends," she said and stood straight under his arm as the turbo-lift decanted them, her circling arm all but carrying him as he tried to make his feet track.

But she made it look good, and the odd looks he got in the hall were more Captain-got-the-girl-again than anything else. Or just It's-the-Captain-welcome-home-sir. He could see that they wanted to run to him, touch him. But they held to discipline and let him move on, never knowing quite how much they had. One day he would have to take a week off and let himself feel what he felt about that.

"Spock," he said near the door. "I have to make it from here."

Her eyes understood and she let him go, but he could feel hair-trigger reflexes at his side ready to catch him again as he cleared his face and set himself to make it.

CHAPTER XXI

James closed his hand over McCoy's as the hand pulled the spray hypo away from his arm. He pointed the Doctor toward the door, and McCoy was there when the Captain came through.

McCoy shoved the shot home without asking and fastened on the arm. The Captain didn't protest being steered to the nearest bed, but he hefted himself onto it with some care and sat with an air of unfinished business.

Spock had turned from the computer to watch, but restrained himself from going to him.

And James thought that he himself was, after all, getting the hang of this link-resonance business. He couldn't seem to screen Kirk's pain out of his own body, but it was he, by God, who had been tuning the link to a thread to keep it away from the Vulcan. Doubtless Spock was allowing it, to keep his own pain to himself. But it was progress.

The Commander had stuck with the Captain to the bed, now turned and came to stand beside James. "All clear," she said in the tone of a report. "A singular performance. The conference of delegates was quite impressed. It will be some time before most of them dare to accuse him of honoring the Prime Directive in the breach again. There is talk of an alliance which would open relations with both Federation and Empire. Omne's people, likewise. A little shell-shocked, but seeing—logic. The delegates will send a commis-

sion to verify the facts of Omne's death, and report
back to us shortly."

"And Sub-Commander S'Tal?" James asked.

"Annoyed," she said, "as is his custom." She smiled
down at him gravely. "He still half suspects that I am
a hostage." She met his eyes in acknowledgement of
fact. "He is—my balance. My advocate of—shooting
'em up. However, I command."

So that was the way of it. 'Tal perhaps more than he
had seemed—

"S'Tal will follow us out to the offshore limit, Captain," she said in a level tone. "As you suggested,
twelve transporter diameters, out of range of transporters and weapons. I suppose we must wait for the
delegates' report. I would feel better if we could head
out at warp speed."

"How much hell have you bought today?" Kirk
asked.

She turned to him with a little lift of her head. "All
there is to buy," she said. "I must now take the Empire apart and put it back together. The decision of
peace or war does not rest in my hands, and I must
reach the point where it does."

Kirk nodded. "That was what I thought. Will 'Tal
back you?"

"No," she said, "but they will have to go through
him to get to me."

Kirk smiled in comprehension and sympathy. "Still,
you will make a time when we can be allies as well as
friends."

"Yes."

"I, too," Kirk said soberly—and then made a rueful
face. "I'm more likely to get talked to death."

"A terrible fate," she said. "On the whole, I would
not trade with you."

Kirk grinned. "On the whole, neither would I."

"On the whole, a satisfactory arrangement," Spock
cut in, "since a trade would be somewhat illogical.
However, I take it we are agreed that for our part the
alliance has already begun, and both Federation and

Empire must be taken apart, if necessary, until both can stand against Omne's threat."

"Agreed, Spock," Kirk said questioningly.

"I recommend we move on to the other problem while you and James are still able to focus on it. You are not concealing from me the need for medical attention and long rest."

So much for that, James thought, suspecting that he looked as sheepish as Kirk. When had Spock ever needed an actual link?

"For once, that's—logical," McCoy said. "Get out of here and let me pack 'em both in."

"I'm afraid that I have to leave before long, Doctor," the Commander said, "or S'Tal really will conclude that I am under duress—or out of my mind."

"Well, excuse me, Commander," McCoy said, puzzled, "but I really can't see that that has much to do with it. You can work out your alliances by viewscreen—later—tomorrow—whenever."

"No, we cannot," she said, looking at Spock.

McCoy thought that he caught her drift. "Oh, well, uh—you and Spock, then, but—"

"No, Doctor," Spock said. "Commander, Captain, we have checked the identity patterns on James. He is absolutely identifiable as James T. Kirk, to the last decimal, beyond doubt or disguise."

Kirk sighed and nodded, looking at James. "What we expected," he said. "You didn't have to go through that."

"Yes, I did," James said, but could not quite bring himself to elaborate.

Spock cut in again. "The implications, Captain. He cannot be hidden anywhere within Star Fleet. Or—except with great difficulty and risk—anywhere within the Federation. I do have one recommendation. With my parents on Vulcan. The Vulcan respect for privacy, the custom of a guest friend—with a sufficient cover story, it would do, and my father would be considerable protection for him. We would have plausible reason to visit—"

The Commander's eyebrows were rising dangerously.

"My God," Kirk said, and his shoulders slumped as
if a weight had finally broken them. He looked at
James with a terrible vista of loss opening before his
eyes. "He—can't. You can't, James. I—couldn't." He
caught his breath. "I—can't. What even makes it—
James? By what right? I can't name one. No difference. But—I'm not willing to give this up." His hand
indicated the ship, perhaps the stars, Spock, McCoy . . .
"How could *you* be? You couldn't." He looked at
Spock. "There has to be another way."

"I see none," Spock said. "The problem is insoluble,
and must be solved. Where there is identity, there is
not, in logic, difference. And yet there is difference
here. Perhaps there is no right, but our assumption—I
believe even James has shared it—has been that there
must be some right of—the original."

"You don't even know about *that*," Kirk said suddenly. "You have only my word that I didn't lose consciousness. You haven't linked with *me*."

Spock's face softened and James felt the sudden
surge of pride. "Not necessary, Jim. No identical Kirk
would lie about that. I doubt the same could be said of
any other man."

Kirk smiled painfully. "I could name one or two. Although—I'm not sure that any man is proof against
this. With time to think about it—" He shook his head.
"I wouldn't trust myself."

"You trust James," Spock said, his eyes pointing
James out, underlining that he had been free on the
Enterprise, was now dressed identically with Kirk.

Kirk grinned as if caught. "Yes, I guess I do." He
flashed a look at James. "Didn't occur to me. I guess it
didn't have to. But the fact remains—"

James nodded. "Given time, possibly. And if there
were no difference."

"But there *is* a difference," the Commander said.
"Listen to you, proposing to dispose of his life. As if

he belonged to you." She faced Spock with fire in her eyes. "He does not, you know. Vulcan, indeed! Is he to grow quivas? Dabble in trillium? Sit on daddy's knee? The first fighting commander of half a galaxy? The first in war—and peace? A man who was willing to sell his freedom for yours—to lose his? The freedom of the stars?"

"If he does not belong to us," Spock said, "to whom does he belong? To you?"

The Commander threw back her head and locked eyes with Spock. "Yes!" she said.

"*What*?" McCoy interjected, and Kirk looked at her, startled.

"I claim him," she said, facing all of them. "I fought for him. I saved his life, and more. By the custom of my people, he is mine if I want him. I want him."

"You mean—" McCoy said, "—you don't mean—you own him? Not literally."

"Why not?" she said. "I challenged for a captive. As it was in the time of the beginning—so is it now: the property of the victor."

"I thought—Spock fought Omne?" McCoy said.

"Once," she said, "—and only because I allowed it to keep this one safe. That was *my* victory, and it makes Spock's victory mine, too. And—I saved this one from damage earlier. I consider that Spock fought for the original. I did, too, but I will not be greedy. It could be an embarrassment of riches."

"Well, *that's* something," McCoy sputtered. "But— you're not serious—"

"Never more," she said. "Spock, can you dispute the right by the custom we share from before the beginning of the division of our peoples?"

"Not by that custom," Spock said grimly. "But I do dispute it."

"Then where is your Prime Directive?" she said. "It is my custom."

"It is *his* life," Kirk said flatly.

"I was wondering if that would occur to anybody,"

James said. He stood up and whirled the Commander to face him. "Don't you think that you ought to ask *me* about that?"

She arched an eyebrow shamelessly. "Only if you will give the right answer."

"Otherwise, just pack me off to your ship?"

"Very possibly," she said. "My people would object to you a good deal less as my captive than as my companion."

"Which place did you offer?" he asked.

"Neither," she said. "There is not a name for the place I would make for you—or for the place you would have to make for yourself. Except as my Human captive—and bed warmer—you could not be with me except as a Romulan, with no man to know what you are, or what you are to me. You would have to rise on your own merit—without benefit of muscle— for you have no muscle there. Not one fight—for you would not only be smashed, you would be discovered, and I with you. I can create an identity for you, but the cover would point to me if you became known. It would have to, but also I will see to it. That would be my protection against your impetuousness. You would risk yourself. You would not risk me."

James felt that his breathing was not quite in order, that there were held breaths in two other bodies linked with his, reverberating in his. "You assume a great deal," he said carefully.

"Am I wrong? Illogical? Presumptuous?" She shook her head. "You want it so badly that you can taste it. The fight. The challenge. The galactic cause cut out to be your size. Rebuilding the Empire at my side. Forging a link to the Federation—creating a peace you could not build in any other way. The continuation of your chosen job. The stars. Your place, your job, your life. Even Spock and Jim from time to time, and not as a—pensioner. Of equal stature in the fight we must all undertake. A chance at Omne—and a chance to present a moving target."

"Out of the frying pan," McCoy said. "Are you both

crazy? He can't pass as a Romulan. An hour maybe—
with a lot of luck, a lucky punch. Crazy even then.
But we didn't know about Romulans then. Couldn't
be sure they had Vulcanoid strength. I found that out
for sure when you were our—guest. Different molecu-
lar structure, bone, muscle—heavier, stronger. A whole
different ball game. He wouldn't last a minute—even
against you."

"He would last considerably less than a minute,"
she said.

"I've lasted with Spock," James said, not bothering
with the difference.

"Even Spock is not a Romulan Commander in full
training," she said. "More muscle—not so much more
as you would think. Less technique. Too many centuries of peace. A certain softness even in Star Fleet."
She shook her head. "But you have lasted for the same
reason you would last with me. He has never fought
you at full strength—and he has pulled you out of
more fires than you can count."

"He has that," James said.

"I have not had to try to keep him alive in the Romulan Empire," Spock said. "And not as a Romulan."

"You were willing to try, when Omne proposed it."

"No option," Spock said. "But I would have made
one, at some point. The prospect of years—decades—of
that— It would be beyond my capacity—and yours."

"It is not beyond mine, Spock. I kept the trust. I
will keep it still. I got him to accept my command. He
will again—and I will keep him safe. Train him. Guard
him. Comfort and keep him. Bend his stiff neck for
him when he needs it." She turned to James and
smiled up at him. "It will be hard on you, harder than
you can imagine. The alpha male of half a galaxy, to
accept command, and mine, and to walk softly? Bluff,
perhaps. Never fight. Know the difference—and never
let anyone else know it. Know—me, and never let anyone else know *that*—for they would have you for
breakfast and use you against me, if they knew—my
price." Her smile was open confession now, and open

challenge. "The man hasn't lived who could do that—but I think he was born today, and—not born yesterday. You know that it will not work if you want only the place, the fight. I do not offer you refuge. But if it is not that—"

"I do not need refuge," James began.

"Wait," Kirk said urgently and came off the bed, shakily, but came to them, came and put his hand on James's arm. "Before you say it— Hell, I can see it. I can see *her*. But your life is here, your friends, family—more." He looked at Spock. "We can't do this to him." He looked back to meet James's eyes. "This is the real crunch of the premise of identical doubles, identical real men. It's a problem even of metaphysics. I don't even see that there's a right of the original—and I want to claim that right so badly that my teeth ache. But you have every right to everything that is mine—life, property, place, command, friends, family, more; to my—memories: yours, ours." He straightened his shoulders as if they would break. "No difference. Yet, I know I can't offer to—go off into the night. How could you?"

James drew a breath to the bottom of his lungs, feeling suddenly that the recognition of the right was a sanction and seal of acceptance, and the straight answer a form of respect which somehow lifted a weight. "I can't," he said with the same respect. "But for me it would not be—night." Somewhere he found a smile, and he touched the Commander's arm. "That has to be the answer," he said, feeling his way. "From the moment of—division—there *is* a difference. A man *is* his memories. Omne died before he would give up the memory of this day. And I would, too. It is mine. Whatever the pain, it is a part of me now—the only part which *is* entirely mine. As yours is entirely yours, whatever we have shared. There are things we have not shared: Spock's acceptance of me, his refusal to regard me as expendable, even after he knew that you lived. The Commander, and how she kept the trust."

James straightened his own shoulders and looked

into the eyes which matched his. "Those are mine. They make the choice possible—not only because it is necessary. Jim—will you take my word?"

Somewhere the matching face found the same smile. "Always, James."

James turned to the woman beside him. "Commander, will you?"

She lifted her head. "Always, James."

He reached up to touch her face, brush her hair back from the swift, lifting ear. "That should be—almost—long enough," he murmured.

Through his fingers he almost thought that he could feel the fire of her mind, and he knew that he could see it in her eyes. "Why don't I know your name?" he said. She would know the one he meant, the private one which Spock had said once still meant "dawn of springtime" in the ancient tongue their peoples had once shared.

"You will," she said, and her eyes promised that he would know much more.

He nodded and turned to the others: Spock—well, there was nothing which could be said to Spock, and nothing which needed to be; Jim—it had been said; McCoy, doing his best not to hover anxiously, and failing.

James grinned. "Take your time with the ear job this time, Bones—" he jerked his head toward the Commander and Spock, "—or we'll never hear the end of it."

"We never will anyway," McCoy grumbled, rallying. But his hand seemed to be shaking and he steadied it on James's shoulder. "There's no pleasing anybody around here." He reached to touch Jim, too. "Thank God," he said.

And he seemed to have gotten the last word again.

But as they moved to go out, James heard Jim say softly, "Stay a moment, Spock."

The Vulcan turned back, and James felt a moment of hollowness which was more than just the medication creeping up on him. But it would be the first moment Jim had had to be alone with the Vulcan. It was Jim's right, their right. They looked natural together, as if they were about to settle down to a command problem.

James made himself walk through the door, and in a moment McCoy had him in a small treatment room and had slapped him with another hypo. He tried not to eavesdrop through the link, but he was aware of Jim's saying something about checking on the message from the delegate commission, which James doubted was what he wanted to say at all.

James found the Commander holding his hand, and his vision was dimming. "I'm in your hands," he murmured a little ruefully.

"Yes," she said with satisfaction.

But as he dropped off, his mind was not entirely with her; it kept drifting off along the link, and he almost thought that he felt another mind entering—Jim? But that had to be an illusion. Still, it would have been Jim's right. . . He couldn't quite feel Jim's body anymore—the drug was soothing, dimming Jim's pain.

James drifted off . . . difference, when he woke there would be even a different face. . .

CHAPTER XXII

When he woke, there was—and James wasn't quite used to it when he went to Jim.

Quite? Would he ever get used to it?

He would, he told himself firmly. The Commander had held a mirror for him, as firmly, and briefed him on how it had been done. She and Spock and Bones—quite a team; she had risen through the ranks as a science officer, too, it turned out. He almost hadn't followed her explanation: it was more than he had bargained for. Not only the ears, the eyebrows, a subtly different face—so subtly that he couldn't entirely pin down the difference. Still his face, but changed by one or two crucial millimeters. And they had found answers to questions he hadn't dared to raise. An injection transplant of bone marrow cells quick-cloned from Spock; they had determined somehow that the Human factors in Spock's blood were compatible with his own, and the Vulcan ones were sufficiently different not to give him the collywobbles or anything—he hoped. She hadn't said collywobbles. She'd said his immunity had been shocked into adapting to the Vulcan elements. And the bone marrow cells would produce enough Vulcan blood cells with their strong pigmentation factors so that he would bleed green. A little off-green, possibly, since it still had to be mostly his blood, and it wouldn't stand medical examination, but it wouldn't give him away at the first scratch or blush.

Then, a subcutaneous injection of Vulcanoid skin-pigmentation-producing cells, also cloned from Spock. And spray-injected all over. But maybe he wouldn't sunburn now.

Hair—a more normal cosmetic process, self-renewing color from the roots out. But they hadn't tried to go dark—more a copper gold color. There were fair Romulans. She said they were "highly prized."

He didn't like the sound of it.

He didn't ask.

He put the thought aside.

It remained to show Jim—the difference.

James moved through the door.

Jim wasn't sleeping—hadn't slept at all, Bones had complained—and of course he could feel now that James was coming, as James could feel that he wasn't sleeping.

But his eyes were closed and he looked drawn; pain still reverberated in the resonance, and it wasn't James's pain.

Jim had put Omne's big black robe on over his uniform. Was he having a chill? But James couldn't feel it.

What he could feel was a kind of waking nightmare, and he knew which one.

Jim didn't turn it off as James crossed to the diagnostic bed, didn't open his eyes—then did both deliberately, looking at the new face.

James put a hand over Jim's eyes, closing them gently. "Don't look at me just yet. Get used to the idea. Finish with the—dream."

"I'm finished with it," Jim said flatly.

"I doubt that either one of us is going to be finished with that for a long time," James said. He softened his voice. "Don't go Vulcan on me now. Haven't we both been deviling a certain Vulcan about admitting to his emotions? And now we both have to admit that we can cry. Hell of a universe sometimes, isn't it?"

Jim laughed in the way that had always been a substitute for crying, and would still do. "Seems to be the only one we've got." He took a breath. "Let me look at you, James."

James took his hand away. He grinned fractionally and saw Jim realize that he had raised his hands to touch his ears where he didn't *have* ears.

But James *did*.

And he saw Jim register that this time they were right for the face—not the hasty cut-and-paste job, hardly better than a makeup job, which McCoy had done in the heat of battle when he had needed Vulcanoid ears. Spock had said that they were not "aesthetically pleasing" on the Human face—and Kirk had known that the Vulcan meant Kirk's face, and was dead serious, for once, in an ear joke.

Kirk couldn't have agreed more. He had looked and felt like an idiot.

But now Jim's eyes said that this Kirk didn't. He looked as if he were born to them and they to him.

James grinned. "Spock and the Commander," he said. "Bones said they designed 'em by computer and stood over him with a club."

Jim laughed. "But of course he takes credit for the artistic touches."

"Indeed."

"Is it—logical—for me to tell you—my compliments?"

"We might both have to admit to being insufferably vain."

Jim grinned. "Enough admissions for one day, already." He sobered. "Almost. I have one for you. But first—Spock— You've been very close to him today. Seen him through hell. Now he has to see you go off into—a good enough version of hell. Your opinion—will he be all right? Between you and me?"

"Between you and me—he will be," James said. "He's as all right as he's going to be for a while—and as all right as he's always been. He's—not so close to me, now. But you would know as well as I. I'd say he's withdrawing a little behind the Great Wall of Vulcan. Needs it, after this day. There's no way he could not react on an elemental level. My emotions—yours. And—he does not even deny it—his own. He descended into hell and brought you back, and me into the bargain. Threaded the labyrinth, fought the monster."

"Legends," Jim said suddenly. "As if the script were written by Omne."

James nodded. "It was. The man of a thousand legends from a thousand worlds. But Spock wrote the ending."

"Except that it will not end."

"No. And Spock will need all the control he owns. He still believes we must express our emotions, and he must master his."

Jim looked up to meet the eyes which no longer quite matched, but matched in this. "We may all need to be Vulcans, for a while."

"Yes," James said. "Take care of him."

Jim smiled. "That's supposed to be *his* act."

James laughed softly. "He'll be hovering over you like a hen with one chick."

Jim shook his head. "He has two chicks now. And—this chick doesn't have to be a Romulan. How are you going to pull that off, by the way? And—what kind of designs does the Commander have on you, exactly?"

James shrugged and grinned. "Beats me. I'm not sure whether she owns me or I own her—or both. Neither. Whatever."

"Doesn't worry you?"

"Worries the hell out of me."

They laughed together.

"Seriously—" Jim said after a moment.

James smiled. "Never more serious. I think the girl finally got the Captain. Or a reasonable facsimile."

"*Reasonable?* You ought to have your head examined."

"I have," James grinned at Jim. "I come by it honestly."

Jim made a rueful face. "I guess you do." He let the face dissolve into seriousness. "James, are *you* all right? No metaphysical qualms? Philosophical hang-ups? Questions about—rights? The difference? You're not just going off into the night?"

James shook his head. "All right—yes, as all right as I'll be for a while. Night—no. For the rest: qualms—I don't think so; questions—sure. Things I don't know how to give up—yes. I'll take some of them with me, find new ones, keep in touch with some old ones." He spread his hands. "I don't know any other logical solution. As for the difference, that may be the one saving grace. I have something you don't have now, something which is mine—and she is my future, not only because she has to be."

Jim looked solemnly into the new face as if wondering whether he couldn't already see a difference that was not surgical. James knew that it was the way Jim would have wanted to take it himself, and that he wondered whether he would have had the courage. Some part of it, they both knew, would be the same kind of putting one foot in front of the other that he had been doing, would have to keep doing for a while. But some of it was more: the sense of a new challenge opening ahead. That, also, Jim understood. That would make it bearable. In time—all right. As all right as it could be.

"I can see it," Jim said and reached out his hand. They locked arms for a moment in more than a handshake.

And then James remembered the Romulan gesture she had taught him. He released Jim's arm and closed his hand into a fist, inviting the crossing of wrists Jim had seen.

There was a signal at the door to McCoy's office and Kirk said, "Come," but he answered the gesture and held it for a long moment before they turned, releasing it.

The Commander bowed her head and her eyes were very bright.

Spock stood quietly very close behind her with the stressed pose of Vulcan control, but with much the same look in the eyes which fastened on the two men who might have been brothers now—even if of different worlds—and not quite, twins.

McCoy stepped quietly around the small island of silence and went to Kirk. "Come on, let's get on with it," he grumbled softly, and his eyes swore at both of them a little. "I agreed with James that you'd want to say good-bye—assuming that anybody can—but you're still my patient and you need a long rest."

"Doctor's orders," Jim said with a sigh of mock resignation, accepting the cussing-out with his eyes and mustering a small grin. "The patient has a complaint." He nodded toward James. "Why is *he* so infernally chipper and healthy?"

He hasn't been through what *you* have, the eyes said accusingly. But McCoy rallied to the old kidding tone. "You can't please anybody around here," he grumped. "Why can't you just tell me that he's gorgeous?"

Jim laughed silently. "I wouldn't touch that one with a pole, Bones. Anyway, that's more in the Commander's line."

"He's gorgeous," she said, rallying too and bowing faintly to Kirk. "He always was." Her eyes took on the slight crinkle of serious mischief. "But now he would make a very satisfactory Romulan—say from one of the matriarch colonies where men are properly treated as delicate creatures and not permitted to fight."

She was at it again: James saw that Jim knew it with perfect clarity, and nonetheless couldn't help bursting out with "*That* isn't going to be your cover story?"

She shrugged, the eyes crinkling. "A logical possibility. I have to stop back to finish a matter which this crisis interrupted. There is such a planet which owes me a princeling as tribute and hostage. And a Warrior Princess there—the Ruler, the terms do not translate—who owes him to me as a debt of honor, and would as soon keep him if she had to hide him in the hills."

"What worries me," James chipped in with a rather feeble grin, "is that I'm not sure that you are kidding."

She arched an eyebrow. "And if I am not?" She moved to stand near James at the foot of the bed. "It would solve a number of problems, you know. You would not be expected to fight, or to exercise with the warrior-men. And no one would think twice about your being under my protection as my property."

It really was not possible to tell whether she was kidding, James thought. Teasing, certainly, but kidding?

"*I* would," James said carefully. "And how would that be any better than being your Human captive and bed warmer? Or—help me to rise in the Empire?"

"Oh," she said innocently, "infinitely more status. A noble tribute-liege is highly prized. An accomplished one is highly regarded. A gorgeous one is to be envied. It is not rare for one to become court favorite and center of intrigue, the power behind the throne—or the command chair."

"Like a—" Jim could not stay out of it and could not finish.

"Woman?" she finished smoothly. "Captive princess? Gift to the conquering ruler? Why not? You have had those customs. Your ancient history even includes matriarchies, and even an occasional society where the roles were truly reversed and men regarded as delicant, vain, talkative, rather silly creatures. I learned a great deal about Human and Vulcan culture while I was with you, and I have been something of a student since."

"We also had slavery," Jim said. "Doesn't prove we haven't outgrown it—or that attitude toward women."

"No?" she said. "Then why object so strongly to some aspects of that role for James? Actually, even our warrior-men have grown surprisingly tolerant of such men from the reversal planets. Consider them rather poor dears to be protected and cherished, but permit them in quite high noncombatant positions. Rather like women in Star Fleet."

"We have women who can fight," Jim said, but looked as if he heard a certain tone of defensiveness in his own voice.

She raised a commenting eyebrow. "You would not care to contend that there is no difference?"

"No," Kirk conceded glumly, "but then, there *is* a difference. Physiological. No matter how much we try to be fair about it, when it's a matter of muscle—"

"Precisely, Captain," she said, and Jim's eyes widened as he saw the trap close. "That is exactly the difference for James, where he's going."

Jim was stumped for a moment, James knew and considered letting his face concede it. But he was prepared to argue for both of them. "No," he said. "That's not all of the difference. Your princeling idea won't work. It's a waste. Illogical—and dangerous. James has all the instincts, reflexes, mind, will, guts, of a fighting man. Bluff. Presence. Whatever it is that makes most men concede without testing. It's your if-you've-got-it-you've-got-to-use-it principle. Try to suppress that and you'll not only cross-circuit all his reflexes, but everybody else's. Subconsciously they'll respond to him half as 'poor dear' and half as alpha male—and he'll really be in trouble."

She raised an eyebrow with a lift of admiration. "Neatly argued, Captain. And I perceive that you do not scruple to call him gorgeous when it counts."

Jim's face flushed, and James wondered whether he, also, was blushing—and was he blushing Romulan?

"Well, it's a—metaphysical problem," Jim said sheepishly. "But what I said is true."

"It is," Spock cut in, "but it is also true that you are a most accomplished actor—both of you."

"Whose side are you on?" James complained.

"Both," Spock said. "I cannot quite imagine you as a 'poor dear,' but your imagination might be equal to the task. There would be major advantages. A princeling who gradually became a power. It is possible that this is a case for thinking outside the reflexes."

"I'm not sure I want to get that far out," James said. "In fact, I'm sure I don't." He looked down at the Commander. "And I'm sure your fertile mind has considered other alternatives."

"You would be surprised at what my fertile mind has considered," she said. "I can write you fourteen scripts for rising through the ranks—provided that I can train you sufficiently to keep your stiff neck unbroken. I can write you seven in which I own you, one way or another."

"I can write you one in which you never will," James said with some heat. "Not if you mean that literally."

"Can you?" she said. "And how literal would that have to be? What if I, too, have some need to own the unownable? It is not your custom, and in truth I am not much of a believer in customs, including my own, but in this case I might make an exception. And in truth we cannot settle this now. Whatever script we choose must be chosen with care, for a lifetime—the public one and the private one. What if the public one is the princeling script? Or the private one different than you can imagine? Would you still come with me? The only real question is whether you can let me walk out that door—without you."

James turned her to face him. "There is another," he said. "Could you walk out without me?"

She lifted her head. "No," she said, "but then I could just pack you off."

McCoy stiffened, but Jim caught his arm with a touch, and James saw the Vulcan straighten almost imperceptibly behind her. She wouldn't, James thought, and was not altogether too damned sure. All her knowledge of Human language and customs which made it too easy to think of her as if she were Human did not, in fact, make her Human. She was an alien from an alien culture, as Spock was, even with his half-Human heritage, but without even that—and possibly without the Vulcan's fundamental civility.

She was a Romulan warrior. And she was herself—one of a kind. Outside the phalanx.

And putting it to James straight that he would have to be outside, too.

James laughed. He looked over her head to the Vulcan, caught Kirk and McCoy with a quick glance. "If it comes to that, I wouldn't count on it," he said. "Or on finding all that too easy even if you had one mere Human in your clutches." He took her face in his hands. "Even when you do have. Poor dear. I'm afraid that you're stuck with me—and I'll have a word or two to say about those scripts. *That* should make it interesting."

Her eyebrows lifted. "*There* we agree."

"*There* will do, for now, will it not?"

"It will," she said, but her back was rather stiff.

James slipped his fingers back into her hair, traced the upswept ears, pulled one of them close to his mouth. "And what," he whispered perfectly audibly, "—what if *I* need to own *you*?"

The stiffness melted. She leaned back and looked up at him with a silent laugh. "Can you afford the luxury?"

"My I ask the price?"

She looked suddenly stricken, and James knew with perfect certainty that she—that all four of them—suddenly heard Omne's heavy voice saying: "The usual. Your soul. Your honor. Your home. Your flag." And all four, even five, knew that that was exactly the price James would now have to offer.

She didn't say it, and James had been caught in the exchange and had not quite seen it coming.

He caught a breath and found a smile. "Done," he said firmly. "But you had better wrap me up and take me with you."

CHAPTER XXIII

The Commander said, "Indeed."

James was bending to kiss her, but she caught his face firmly between her hands, her paired fingers touching his temples and the tips of his upswept ears.

The customless kiss from between the stars had been right for the man who had been Captain Kirk.

But this was her innocent princeling, whatever the script, who would come to her on her own ground, where the way of the beginning prevailed, and he would come in her way.

She held him with her strength and touched him with the most ancient kind of mind-link, and not with the restraint of the Vulcan.

The Vulcan was still there with his restrained link. That would not do, not for much longer, but it would do for now, and it did not deter her. James caught his breath under the new touch, and she could even feel, through the resonance, Jim catching his. That did not deter her, either. There were precious few secrets around here today.

But she kept the touch light. There were still things which would be private.

But for this she would not wait.

It was more than a kiss, and he trembled under it, but she felt his own bedrock strength and it was sufficient to meet her.

She was not quite breathing, either.

There was not a breath in the room, not even from the Doctor.

And into that silence came—no sound, but a sudden sense of presence.

It raised hackles down her spine, and she turned to see the silent shimmer of a transporter forming the massive, behemoth outline which could only be one man out of a galaxy.

Omne.

It was not possible that he could be here, beyond all transporter range.

But she did not consider the impossibility.

She launched herself in a flat leap to close with him in the instant when he would still be helpless in the transporter beam. The Vulcan wore a phaser. He could stun her with Omne while she blocked Omne's weapon. Spock would see the necessity.

She crashed into the great bulk with a body block and chop to the throat, while her other hand smashed down the gun arm.

Except that the corded arm barely moved—and for a long split instant she could feel the heat of Omne's body, as if time had stopped. She knew that the Vulcan was drawing, James and Jim trying to move—

And in the same split instant Omne caught her with a roar and slammed her against the Vulcan, crashing them both to the floor.

She knew dimly through white pain that the slam had been hard enough to kill them both if they had been Human.

James was charging Omne.

'No, James!' she shot through the link, and came up off the floor.

But it was already too late. He had launched a savage kick at Omne, possibly the only kind of blow the Human could give which had a chance.

But Omne absorbed the sickening crunch of James's feet and caught James out of the air.

Jim was flying from the couch, but a swipe of Omne's other arm tossed Jim against her—not with such force.

The Vulcan was diving past her, propelled by murder.

Omne caught him with a knee in the ribs, which exploded in the link. Still his hands went for Omne's throat, but a smash of the giant's arm felled him to his knees, and a kick toppled him.

McCoy was there from somewhere, with less muscle, but with desperate courage.

Omne felled him with a cuff.

She was putting Jim aside and going in again, but he moved with her.

Then Omne said, "Cease!" and they saw that he had an arm locked around a struggling James from behind, and a phaser leveled at her. Not the revolver, which the giant still wore in his holster, but an advanced design of phaser. Impossible to tell whether it was set to stun or kill.

She kept going, knowing that the first moment of explosive action was all they had, all they would ever have.

Omne could transport out in the next moment with James.

But if they all kept coming—

Jim was at her shoulder.

She went for the eyes, the nerve center under the great jaw—trying to be careful of the Human between.

Omne caught her with a backhand of the fist holding the phaser.

She had not dreamed of being hit with such power. She went down, fighting with every Vulcanoid skill for consciousness, trying to scissor her legs to cut Omne's legs from under him.

But he was planted like a two-legged tree.

He caught Jim with a gentler swipe, brushing him off like a sand gnat, and dropping him almost solicitously on Spock as the Vulcan tried to rise. Spock rolled Kirk off and kept coming. Omne caught him with a boot to the jaw.

Then Omne stepped back a pace with the lightness of a dancer, and he had his arm locked around James's throat in a chancery strangle, slowly subduing the Human who had still been aiming blows and kicks against the great body and legs. Omne put the phaser to James's temple.

James's consciousness faded to a pounding blackness, and the Commander rapped out again, 'James, stop!'

And this time she was obeyed—possibly because he could do nothing else.

Nor could any of them. She or Spock might still have made a move, but a phaser stun effect at point-blank range might easily kill James—or Omne might break his neck.

It was not as if she or Spock could fight with a clear field. There were the Humans. The link and resonance reverberated with their pain, and it had to be admitted that there was a Vulcan and Romulan contribution too.

She tasted the bitterness of defeat, and it was not as strong as the metallic taste of panic.

Omne had not eased the strangle.

She came to her knees. "Stop!" she said, and it had the tone of a plea.

"How do you ask?" Omne rumbled.

"I—beg," she said.

She saw the wolf smile appear on Omne's face. "I believe it is for yourself."

"Yes," she said proudly.

"And you, Spock?"

"Yes," Spock said.

Omne felt James sagging against him and finally eased the strangle. James wilted and would have dropped like a sack, but the giant held him.

"Murderer—you've killed him!" McCoy said, coming off the floor. "Let me—" His hands reached for James and his voice had almost the tone of hysteria. She was thinking with a trace of pity that the poor Human was entitled: only the link told her that James was not dead.

And then she saw the palmed spray-hypo going for Omne's shoulder.

She didn't let a flicker of reaction reach her face.

But Omne moved with that omniscient sense he seemed to have—or with the reflex of pulling James away—perhaps both, and he saw the hypo.

He chopped the phaser down on McCoy's wrist, and the Doctor choked on a scream as the hypo clattered.

Then the phaser was back at James's ear, and he was stirring slowly.

Omne laughed.

"So even the good Doctor is full of surprises. I trust you appreciate mine."

He looked fresh as a new-minted coin, shockingly alive, vital, magnetic, his presence filling the room, as if he had truly been reborn.

The Phoenix from the flames.

Black Omne.

He was truly the first, she thought, the first immortal—back from the other side of death.

Of course he would have to come to celebrate.

"We've been expecting you," she said, coming to her feet, banishing pain.

He laughed again. "I hardly think so, my dear. But you should have. When will you learn that you will never know my capabilities until they are used against you?"

Spock was on his feet, but slow, the half-healed ribs gone again, the hands, the knees—the pain blinding in the link until he tuned it down. Jim was steadying the Vulcan, the Human less hurt himself this time, but reeling from the choking of James and from the cumulative shocks and injuries of the day, from the brute shock of Omne's overwhelming presence. McCoy was sagging against a couch and nursing a wrist as if it were broken.

They were a sorry crew to face this mint-condition monster.

Of them all, only she had been remotely fit to fight after this day, and there was a point where plain brute muscle and heft told, and that incarnate, undying will which was Omne.

But her will was no less certain. Mind and will would have to serve now. Hers. Get him talking; keep him talking. Where was Mr. Scott with his intruder alert? Would he have sense enough to know that there could be only one intruder? Yes. And what would he do?

"The Empire would pay high for a transporter of that range," she said.

Omne dismissed it. "Let us not waste time talking of hardware, my dear. There is only one piece of hardware in the galaxy which has any real price, from this day forward—and I own that, as well."

She bowed her head in acknowledgement. "True. It is a complete success. A triumph. Let us negotiate *that* price."

He laughed the wolf laugh. "My dear, do not attempt flattery. I am not in need of it. I will boast of the process myself, if I wish."

"And I will acknowledge, if I wish, that you took the very last chance, and won the final victory."

She had to deliver the acknowledgement in the tone of a battering ram, but she saw it reach the black eyes.

"Yes," Omne said simply. "I did."

Jim drew up close beside her, but he did not touch the moment, nor did the Vulcan, and James stayed quiet, trying to still even his mind, not to joggle her elbow.

The confusion of links and resonance was a distraction, full of pain and James's sub-voice thoughts, in which the only hopeful theme was: Scotty. But she would not have given up one gossamer thread of the link for all the princelings in the Empire; the link might have to lead her to hers.

"You are the first," she said to Omne. "The Phoenix. The Fire-Dragon."

"Yes," he said, accepting the acknowledgement, and then he swept it away with a slight ironic smile. "You discount James?"

"James did not die."

"No." The great dark eyes brooded for a moment over the memory; they were more unfathomable than ever, layer upon layer of depth, like obsidian gone transparent. Was there something new in the eyes, now—as if death had burned something to great clarity? "You were almost right, Commander. Of all men I would not die—and of all men, I was the only one who would. But I was not beaten. I was the man who would die first—and did."

"So," she said slowly, "you found a recording of our discussion in the control room?"

"Certainly, my dear. All of the monitor screens record automatically. This whole day is safe on storage cubes."

She felt Jim stir uncomfortably beside her.

Well, it could not be helped. "I trust I did not omit too many possibilities?" she said with a trace of challenge.

"Dozens," Omne said. "Hundreds."

She smiled fractionally. "You will doubtless fill me in."

Omne smiled, as if indulging her, as if he knew all about what she was up to, and could afford the luxury. And beneath the smile she saw suddenly the savage hate which had exploded in the fight and not been dissipated. It was leashed now. Omne had not forgiven them their victory, or his death.

"You are seeing only the test of the process against love," Omne said. "Consider the tests against hate, evil, weakness, power-lust, Human frailties. Consider even the test against strength and decency. You have had advantages, you know. Jim and James are quite extraordinary men—and they had quite extraordinary help." Omne looked at her, at Spock. "But picture two kings, emperors, presidents waking up on any one day to find—two of them. One could not count on our two originals' nobility. Even they barely made it. But consider: what if such a pair did not even know which was the original? Each would have to fight for his rightful place. The other would be an imposter—who was certain that he was real. What if there were no Vulcan friend, no telepath who knew them to establish identity? And what if there *were* such a friend? Which would he choose—and how? How would one of them choose to leave him? Suppose even today, my dear, that you had not been here to offer another path to James?"

"The thought has occurred," she said with effort.

"It is only one possibility," Omne said. "There are countless permutations, combinations, surprises, elemental uses. Possession. Exploration of metaphysical problems. There is simple personal survival."

"At a price," she said grimly. "Doubtless also surprising." Where was Mr. Scott? How long could she stall?

"Certainly," Omne said. "I am full of surprises. Are you trying to conceal from me one of your own? For example, that it is long past time for the Captain's Mr. Scott to have sounded intruder alert, if he detected my transporter? Therefore he is either trying to take silent action, in the hope of which you are stalling, or I have yet another capability which will come as a surprise to you."

She shrugged microscopically, not betraying the sinking sense that Omne was ahead of them on all points. Did Scott even know? "If you have named my game," she said, "it is still the only game in town. Although we might still arrange one or two other surprises. But you have come. You wanted to say to us: *I live.* You might thank us for that—at least, thank the Captain. We did not destroy you when we could. You owe a debt."

Omne shook his head. "I am not responsible for missed opportunities or misguided nobility—or, especially, for rationalizations of elemental needs." He turned to Jim. "One innocent life, Captain? Shall I tell you the real reason why you did not destroy the planet?"

Kirk nodded. "I named it. But tell me what you think."

"Because it *is* immortality, Captain. You could not bear to close the door on the defeat of death. You will find that you have sold your soul for it—and the galaxy."

Kirk straightened, and she saw that it was true—on some deepest level, true. She could feel it in James's mind, too. Kirk's head lifted. "It *is* immortality," he said. "You could have been honored for it forever. But it is you who have sold your soul. Yes, I want the defeat of death." He gestured toward the stars. "What else are we out here for? To learn, to know, to push back the limits, to—love. Who would see love die? No, I didn't close the door. I would be willing to live with Pandora's box—and Hope. But not with immortality as a weapon in your hands. I have not sold the galaxy. We will fight you."

"You have tried that, Captain," Omne said, indicating their defeat.

"We are not finished. Who are you that we should quit against you?"

"Omne," the giant said simply.

Kirk nodded. "You are that—and we have not quit. You have lost today. You met love, and you couldn't break it."

"It will break *you*," Omne said. "Captain, you wanted the process, and you did not want it for the galaxy, but for yourself."

Kirk stood very still. She could feel the effort in his body. "I wanted it," he said. "But I have lived without it before."

He stood as if waiting for a blow to fall; she saw the hate flare again in the obsidian eyes and the great arm tighten across James's chest.

James gasped and Kirk set his teeth, and for a moment she thought that the giant would break from the

pose of studied calm and come to smash—which was
perhaps what Kirk had intended.

It would break the deadlock. Get Omne out of his
secure position with his hostage and his back against
the wall, commanding the doors.

Of course. Scott might be outside, monitoring, only
waiting for a chance. And if not—she was not out of it,
and Kirk would not count himself out, or James, even
the Vulcan with his broken ribs.

She set herself to move.

But the giant was master of himself. He smiled the
wolf smile. "I am not to be drawn, Captain. I chose
you for that very capacity. It is what made you a fit
subject for the first test. But you have lived without
immortality when it did not exist. Now it does exist,
and you have tasted it."

There was a long moment of silence. She could feel
the weight of it in the link. Each of them had lived for
a long time on the final frontier of death, and still
dared to love. It had been necessary. It was the nature
of the universe, and what man, what all intelligent life
had had to live with, always. And it had always been
unendurable, and endured.

But now it was *not* the nature of the universe.

She undertook to speak for all. "We would give anything for it—except what we are."

"So say you all?" Omne said, and his eyes were
darkly impressed as he felt the weight of common as-
sent like a solid unity among them. Even McCoy
lifted his head and met the black eyes with a searing
look of loathing and icy, bleak pride—he who fought
death on his own ground and too often lost, and
would fight again.

Omne nodded. "So you will not, after all, quite sell
soul, flag, fortune, and sacred honor?"

"We will not sell what makes love possible," the
Commander said.

"But *that* is the price of the Phoenix," Omne said. He
laughed then, darkly. "And you will pay. Today your
lambs speak together. Your wolves will come to me

one by one, in silence, as will the wolves of the galaxy. You will come when the strain of living with death and love and the knowledge of eternal life becomes too much. Commander, you have touching plans for taking James into the Romulan Empire. What will you do on the day when your gorgeous, delicate princeling fails to bow his stiff neck and is discovered? Or perhaps even is betrayed—it could be arranged, you know—and is thrown into the dungeons of the Empire?"

Yes, what? she asked herself, fighting down the feeling of sickness. But aloud she focused only on the detail. "We have spoken of a princeling only here. Are we to assume that you have been following that conversation, too?"

"But of course," Omne said smoothly. "That also is on tape. I must say, it has been my one disappointment in you. You had ample opportunity to know that I could tap into your intercom system. You have been rather leisurely. You might have done me the honor of moving out at warp eight. But I suppose that you can be forgiven a certain lingering shock."

She grimaced. In fact the delay had worried her. But she had seen no means of avoiding it. The problems had to be worked through—political, medical— even the problems of metaphysics, even the emotions; the Vulcan had known it as well as any of them, perhaps better. "We were entitled," she said. "However, we had our reasons. And we have said nothing which you could not infer from the plain fact of James in the Empire."

Omne nodded. "Except perhaps for the delightful picture of the princeling. You have been practically shellmouths on the subject of how you propose to cope with *me*. It is a problem, you know. I cannot, of course, permit the alliance of Federation and Empire."

"You cannot prevent it," she said. "You yourself have forged the bond."

Omne nodded. "That I must undo, before the welding becomes too solid. It was a risk I took. It was nec-

essary to test the process against the best the galaxy
had to offer." He bowed fractionally to them. "I had
not fully reckoned with how good the best could be."

They all stood carved in stone.

She understood it only as she did it, standing without even a nod in return. And she saw the understanding and the hate flare in Omne's eyes. He could accept their acknowledgement. They could not grant the
value of his.

He locked down to savage control and nodded
slowly. "I will not say that it was necessary to test
your best with my worst. But because I did, you may
not have taken my galactic purpose seriously enough.
You, Commander, could still believe that I would
fight you to take over the galaxy. I am far more dangerous than that. I have no ambition to be a petty
dictator—even of a galaxy. You will learn to your cost
that I genuinely am an advocate of freedom—no matter how hell-busted or weather-beaten the fragile
ideal may be, or the outlaw who defends it."

He looked at them gravely, and for a moment they
all must have seen the enduring purpose in the black
eyes: the lie he had wanted them to speak which was
the truth a certain man had learned when love died.
For a moment she thought that she saw that man's
face in the face of Omne: a younger face, alien—and,
somehow, without sin. Was that what Omne had
been?

He put the face away, as he must have put it away
long ago.

But the grave look remained for a moment. "The last
thing I can permit is your alliance, if I must kill you to
prevent it. Nor was it any part of my plan to give a
Kirk to each side. Nor will I."

He tightened his hold on James. She stiffened.

"You have no Kirk to give," James said through his
teeth.

Omne laughed. "But I *have*. You are created life:
property, mine—and—the property of the victor."

"You lost," James grated out.

Omne chuckled. "Come, princeling, it was you who told me that force is not an answer to argument. Do you now wish to contend that it is? But I have won on that count, too. I died for the privilege. However, we can have many such arguments—for the next thousand years. I really cannot loose you on the galaxy; one Kirk is already an embarrassment of riches. He will yet weld empires together wall to wall across the galaxy, leaving not even a hole in the wall for freedom—or a wolf loose in the galaxy. Except, of course, me. But I will be wolf enough."

"Omne," Kirk cut in, "are you not wolf enough—or man enough—to face two of us?"

Omne smiled. "Why, yes, Captain. You may come, too, if you wish. I am still giving some thought to taking the original—or both of you. In time you would not only be mastered, but would see my idea of freedom. I could use a Kirk or two who did."

Kirk shook his head. "Not in a thousand years."

"We would have forever," Omne said gravely, and then smiled. "However, just at the moment your disappearance might raise inconvenient questions about the process. The disappearance of James will not, since he does not exist."

"The disappearance of James would raise more than a question," the Commander said flatly.

Omne grinned. "I cannot tell you how you terrify me, my dear." He shrugged. "To whom would you appeal for help? Your Empire? The Federation? To what Geneva convention? *Who* is being held prisoner, you say? Captain Kirk? But he is on the *Enterprise.* A Captain Kirk who has elegant ears and looks rather like a Romulan princeling? But, my dear Commander, are you certain you have not been overworking?"

"I would not require help to take you apart," she said, but in fact she knew that he was right. Once he was back behind his shields— She tried to picture arguing with Omne's trustees, with the conference of delegates, for permission to search the planet. No. He was not leaving with James—certainly not without her.

There had to be a moment when she could at least throw herself into the transporter effect with them.

It was a conclusion her whole body had reached long ago, she realized, finding herself posied for it.

'No,' James said silently through the link, but she did not argue.

"She *has* help," Kirk said quietly, stepping forward to face Omne. "The alliance has begun. Nothing will break it, or us. As for James, what I said about the right of one innocent life goes for us, too. We have the right to defend ourselves and each other. You may think that under no circumstance can we do anything to risk revealing the process. Wrong. We can if we must. It would be a grave step, but we are prepared to face the consequences. Under no circumstance are we prepared to surrender any one of us to death or captivity or your games—not one of us, not anyone else dear to us, not anyone under our commands, and, so far as we are able, not anyone at all."

Omne lifted a black eyebrow dangerously. "Captain, you require another lesson in mastery."

Kirk shook his head. "You require the lesson." He straightened further and stood very quiet, but there was an electric quality in the quietness, a sense of crackling power perhaps even to match Omne's. She looked at him in astonishment. Had she missed something? This was not the look or tone of defeat, but nothing had happened. Had his mind snapped? Did he have some sick need to reassert himself against Omne? But it was not the tone of madness.

"Omne," he said, "yours is not an innocent life. For what you have done—to name only kidnapping—death is the ancient penalty. For what you have done which cannot be named by ancient or modern law, death is not too great a penalty—even for an immortal. For what you *will* do, death is not even penalty enough. We have no forgiveness. The—wolves—here would like to tear out your throat. *I* would. But we have made some effort to claw our way out of swamp and jungle. We cannot offer you trial—or treatment, if we supposed you to be insane. It is not our way to execute in the manner of murder. But you have placed yourself outside our law, and outside the pale. One thing, however, we recognize: your achievement, and the mind which was capable of it. There is one way in which you can still be honored for that, and in which the achievement can take its proper place in the galaxy. We offer no forgiveness or pardon, but I offer amnesty on one sole condition: that you surrender the process and agree never to use it privately, on pain of death, while we in this room, including you, become a commission to oversee its careful, proper introduction to the galaxy. I offer amnesty, honor, life—as against death with finality. Choose now."

Omne heard him out with the incredulous look of an astonishment too profound even for anger.

The giant laughed, roared. "You offer *me* amnesty? You act as if you had the power to offer me anything? To threaten me?"

Kirk stood unmoved. "I ask you to believe that I do. I offer you one chance, Omne. Choose."

"Captain," Omne said with exaggerated patience. "I just mopped up the floor with all of you. I assure you that I shielded my beam so that Mr. Scott will not have detected it. I am aware that you are stalling, but I would appreciate it if you would do it in a more plausible manner. You really cannot draw to a pair and then bluff like a pat hand. Bad poker, Captain."

"You hold the dead man's hand, Omne, against—four of a kind." Kirk shifted fractionally. "Did you really suppose that we would stay here like a sitting target? That Spock couldn't calculate the probable real range of your transporter? That I couldn't make a pretty fair off-the-wall estimate? That I couldn't read you well enough to know that you would have to come? We couldn't come into your hole after you, but we could lure you out of your hole. What better bait than ourselves—the only ones to whom you could show what you are? You've been lured, Omne. You've been had. We're pleased you accepted our invitation to crash the party."

Omne laughed again. "It would be like inviting a Fire-Dragon to a tea party. I trust you have enjoyed the company. Captain, do you really suppose that I didn't consider even that possibility? But it is not my temperament to skulk in my hole. And I took the precaution of speed-monitoring all your tapes, with spot checks of the bridge and other key areas. You have not had an opportunity to set anything up."

"Come, Dragon—do you suppose that we didn't consider *that* possibility?" Kirk smiled savagely. "You have had ample opportunity to know of our capability with the mind-link. Mr. Spock and I set something up: *you.*"

It was the conclusion she had reached herself—the two of them when they were alone—and she flared murder at the Vulcan through the link, understanding now his preternatural quietness and his shielding even from James, which she had taken for mere restraint. 'Allies!' she sent scaldingly.

Spock remained obdurately silent, even in the link.

'Trust him, them,' James sent, but she could feel his hurt and anger too: had they set something up without him, without her, or were they—bluffing?

"Bluff, Captain," Omne said, but his voice lacked a fraction of an edge of certainty.

Suddenly his arm moved to lock across James's throat and his hand moved up to touch James's face in the position of the Vulcan mind-touch. But Omne was not a telepath—

Then she felt the great, dark mind reaching into James's mind, a sudden, black swiftness—and with it elements of a more familiar mind, sunlit but with its own shadows of conflict and great power leashed to discipline: the Vulcan's mind; Spock.

Then, even as she fought to shield James she understood: Spock had been linked to Omne when he died, and Spock also had shared the ultimate fear of death.

His—emanations—had also radiated, and been re-corded, intermingled with Omne's. Spock's powers, his knowledge, his capabilities—Omne's now. Omne's. The danger—

The dark mind beat at her, at James's mind, like great black wings, and she sheltered the Human and beat the preying blackness back, back—but its power was awesome.

Then it was gone as swiftly as it had come, and she knew that it had found no plot in James's mind or in hers.

"Bluff, Captain," Omne said again with certainty, dropping his hand to catch James more firmly as he sagged.

Kirk swayed, but he grated out, "That, also, we had to know."

Omne's eyes narrowed. In spite of the negative ev-idence of James's mind, he was beginning to believe. Kirk's certainty radiated in the room. Omne shrugged. "A perfectly logical extension of the capability. Minds locked in death. Fascinating. I would have told you in time. Perhaps even this time. It will mean that I will be able to anticipate your every move."

Kirk nodded. "Unless we are able to—think outside the phalanx. We just did."

Omne chuckled. "I am almost tempted to let James go. It would be most entertaining to watch the four of you trying to think outside the phalanx—watch the Commander and James trying to build a life to-gether, arguing about scripts and princelings, trying to remodel the Empire, and knowing always that my shadow stands over them; that they may find me around any corner, blocking any plan; that they must try to snatch happiness from the teeth of terror—and know that the blow may fall at any moment. You and Spock, also, knowing that, and knowing how well I know you. You are all worthy opponents." Omne smiled the wolf smile and straightened, pulling James closer. "But because you are, I cannot permit myself the luxury. I must have an ultimate hostage against you. Captain, I regret that you do not seem to be hostage for the Commander. I believe that James *is*—even for you."

"He is," Kirk said, "but you will not have him."

"Forgive me, but I do not see how you will stop me," Omne said urbanely. "And I do not believe I will stay to see you try. I might kill someone. And you are all so noble and so vastly entertaining. If you will excuse me—"

"You reject amnesty?" Kirk said in the tone of command—and finality.

Omne laughed. "Of course. Does the wolf accept amnesty from the lambs?"

Kirk shook his head almost sadly. "No more than the—shepherds—can let the wolf prey." He drew himself up and seemed suddenly to tower like a monument to justice. "Then—die, Omne."

His hand flicked in a gesture to Spock. " 'Now, Mr. Scott,' " the Vulcan said aloud and in the link. 'Commander, get James away—' But at the same moment Omne reached into James's mind and with the Vulcan's own power snapped the link to the preoccupied Vulcan before Spock could move to defend it. Spock's and James's agony flared in the last of the link—and then Omne reached for *her* link with James. She fought—

Suddenly there was a hum and she saw Omne's phaser shimmer in a peculiar-looking transporter effect. Federation transporters couldn't *do* that—could they? The transporter could have taken James's head off.

But she didn't question. She moved to get James away, even as he fought to free himself. But this time she had an instant to gain balance and she moved with the full training of a Romulan Commander, slashing her bladed hands into the nerve centers of the great bull shoulders and in a continuation of the same movement snatching James out of the momentarily weakened arm.

It left Jim Kirk facing Omne, and Omne still had the holstered six-shooter.

She swung James behind her and started to move again.

But Kirk had torn open the great black robe and he wore another of the old guns—McCoy's—holstered under it.

His hand found the gun with unerring precision and with the speed of thought, even as Omne went for his.

There was a roar, and even she with Romulan senses was not certain which gun had spoken, or whether both with one voice.

But there is no mistaking the impact of a large-calibre bullet at close range.

It blasted Omne back against the wall with an impact which shook it, while his gun clattered against the wall and fell.

And she saw Kirk on his feet, the Vulcan's hands closing on his shoulders and going white.

But it was only a moment, and then they were both moving to Omne, while she scooped up the fallen gun with the hand which was not holding James—almost holding him up.

She did not trust the great bull vitality of the dark giant, even against that doom.

Incredibly the great tree-trunk legs were still holding Omne up against the wall, although there was a hole in his chest and a wide splatter of blue green blood behind him.

The black eyes blazed with unquenchable life, and with—astonishment.

McCoy moved in with his scanner, shook his head.

"This time you are away from your equipment," Kirk said very quietly. "It is—final."

Omne looked at them, at the faces one by one, as if to remember them forever. "The game of gunsmoke, Captain," he rasped. "It is—fitting."

Kirk nodded. "I thought so."

Omne turned to Spock. "Look in your mind, Vulcan, for what is unlocked by the word *Omnedon*."

Spock tuned inward with an abstracted look. In a moment he said, "I shall mourn—Omnedon."

Omne smiled the wolf smile against a grimace of agony. "Never mourn Black Omne."

"*I* shall," Kirk said. "The mind. The giant. Not the wolf, but the man who defeated death."

Omne laughed, breathlessly, without sound. "Remember that. Quickly, now, how did you transport the phaser?"

"An antibiologic circuit," Spock said. "An adaptation of—pest control. We had to assume that you would be armed and might hold one of us. The circuit was reversed to take metal and leave flesh—not to take a hand off, or an ear."

Omne nodded as if he understood completely, as perhaps he did, with what he knew from Spock's mind. "Fascinating. It would require fine tuning. Time. One could calculate the interval." He nodded again with a gesture oddly like a Vulcan with curiosity satisfied. The pain caught him. "Why didn't you shoot me in the first moment?"

"Nobility," the Commander said. "I cannot tell you how tired I am of nobility."

James caught the blaze in her mind at the risk to him, and there was a flame in his mind, too, and the picture of her charging Omne's phaser. He pulled himself to the bleak control of understanding. "Even Omne had to have his chance. Or it's still—jungle."

Omne laughed silently to her. "Nobility. My dear, I'm afraid you are stuck with it." He looked at James.

"They will not be stuck with looking over their shoulders for *you*," Kirk said. "Nor will the galaxy. We could not have that."

"You see, noble Captain," Omne breathed, "there was a price for which you would do murder."

"Yes," Kirk said. "But I did not."

"No," Omne said, as if it were loaded with more than agreement.

"He has defeated you, Omne," the Vulcan said, "with more than muscle. He is the man you might have been—and for what you might have been, I could wish that the price had not been so high."

Omne smiled. "You have much yet to learn about the man I might have been, and am—and about the price of the Phoenix."

McCoy straightened with the scanner. "I'm sorry," he said in the manner of the doctor. "I can't do anything for you. It is final."

And indeed the light in the great black eyes seemed to be fading.

Omne laughed.

It was an undying echo of the great bull roar, and the smile on the dying face was the smile of the wolf.

The Commander felt a chill investigate her spine, and she drew James closer.

Omne caught his breath on the last note of the laugh.

"Is it?" he said.

Then his hand caught at some small device on his belt.

The obsidian eyes went opaque.

The great body began to topple like a tree.

Then it vanished in silence.

CHAPTER XXIV

McCoy turned to the four.

There was only one question in all the eyes, Vulcan, Romulan, Human.

Is it final?

Nightmare, McCoy thought.

"He was dead," he said aloud. "I'd swear it. Final."

"Logic, Doctor," the Vulcan said, not as baiting but with the tone of an old nightmare, or a new one. He bent stiffly to pick up the small device which had dropped from Omne's belt. "The process works from a transporter effect. We do not know that the 'emanations' cannot also be beamed as transporter-coded information. It would be the logical solution."

"But—he was already dead," McCoy said doggedly.

"Was he?" Spock was examining the device.

"Spock—it's not—a belt recorder?" Kirk said rather hollowly, looking at the little device as if it might contain the soul of Black Omne.

"No," the Vulcan said, "although he might have worn one—clipped to the back of his belt, concealed in a boot. We do not know how far he had gone with miniaturization. But it may have been simpler than that. He could easily devise an open transporter tracer-beam, a signalling device—"

"Spock," McCoy said irritably, "what the devil are you getting at? And what is that you've got there?"

Spock looked up with bland Vulcan innocence. "Doctor, it is—a dead-man switch."

"What?"

"A device which depends upon the continuing life of its user for its operation," Spock explained patiently. "The earliest mechancial versions stopped a steam locomotive if its operator died. Considering Omne's strength, this one did approximately the same."

"Spock, *will* you talk English?" McCoy grumbled.

"I believe I *did*, Doctor." Spock's tone was infinite weariness.

The Commander took the open device from the Vulcan's nerveless hands, looked at it. "Gravity operated with a drop of mercury," she translated. "Simple. So long as Omne stayed alive and on his feet, it sent out a signal to the transporter beam not to take him. If he died—or even if we had overpowered him or stunned him—it would signal the beam to lock on." She looked at Kirk, at the others.

"He left it for us," Kirk said slowly, "to raise the question: Is it?"

"Precisely," Spock said.

"So," James said, "we have to face that question again."

"Not quite," Kirk said. "There was no question before. He would not have killed himself if he were not virtually certain. But we *did* surprise him. Here, at the edge of his transporter range, away from his equipment, dead, we believe, before the beam took him—" He straightened. "We might just have done it."

"Or might not," McCoy murmured, looking at the four and seeing a long vista. Never look behind you. Something might be gaining on you.

Omne.

"We will not know," Spock said, "until and unless he is ready—if he does live. This time he will go to ground. The delegates' commission reported only moments before he came; they verify the death of Omne; his estate is in the hands of trustees; he is mourned by those to whom he gave refuge, and in some quarters, where short memories will forget or disbelieve small matters like kidnaping, he may yet be mourned as a martyr to freedom.'

Kirk frowned. "But you said *you* would mourn Omnedon. What was all that, Spock?"

"One day I will tell you all of it," Spock said. "Omne wanted to be known, to the last. Omnedon was his name. It unlocked a memory I did not know I had from him. It must have been part of the final exchange at the moment of death—a memory he had virtually locked away from himself." Spock's eyes looked distant. "There was a time when Omnedon laughed, not with the sound of the wolf. He was a man of power, but not of force. A giant—not only of size, and not of evil. He was—the Alexander of his world, but not by conquest—almost—the Surak, uniting warring realms under a philosphy of peace and freedom. When the Federation came—a very early contact—he embraced it. The science, the technology, the diversity, the chance at the stars. He became a leading scientific mind, and the first advocate of bringing the benefits of change to his people. He ran into the stone wall of custom. Finally it broke him, and his world, and he never forgave himself. It was *he* who was the leading breaker of the Prime Directive."

Spock returned as if from a distance. He looked at Kirk. "But what he did not forgive himself—or you, was that he reached a point when he—quit."

Kirk was silent for a long moment. "He has learned that lesson," he said finally. "He didn't quit today, even against death. He will not quit again."

"No," Spock agreed. "Perhaps that is what he wanted to learn from you."

"You're talking about him as if he didn't die," McCoy said.

Kirk almost smiled. "Even if he did, he didn't quit. I wish we could go back and reach—Omnedon. The man *was* a giant. Or—is. There aren't very many of them."

"He was a monster," McCoy growled.

"That, too." Kirk made a small movement, as if to shake something off. "All right," he said in the command tone, "we just have to get on with it. If he lives, he is a more serious enemy even than we knew. A conqueror with designs on dictatorship we might more easily fight. But the most sinister swindle in all history has always been to claim to advocate freedom—at the point of a gun. And the most dangerous man is the man who believes in his own swindle. Now we have a man who believes, and a man who will cram his version of freedom down the galaxy's throat—at the point of his process. Moreover, now he has Spock's powers. Superlatively dangerous. We must do what we planned—but in spades, and never knowing fully whether we may find Omne around any corner. The alliance—"

"You have betrayed it at the first opportunity," the Commander said savagely. "Secrets. By what right did you risk James's life without my knowledge or consent?"

Kirk turned to her wearily but solidly. "Commander, you are absolutely right. We had not that right, nor the right to act without James's consent. I undertook to answer for his, and I—usurped, if you like—the right to answer for yours, temporarily. To set the trap, we had to stay within reach. It was always possible that he would grab one of us and go—or grab one of us and hold him, as he did James. If we could not stop him or stun him in the first moment, as we hoped, we had to be able to keep the secret from him, keep him talking, until Scotty had time. Spock recognized the possibility that Omne had acquired some of his knowledge and powers. If he had read one of us too soon— However, it was our intention to tell you, as soon as the trap was fully set and Spock had a chance to link with you without arousing suspicion."

"Sometime next year?" she said unforgivingly.

Kirk smiled ruefully. "In fact, we might already

have done it if you hadn't mixed up my head with that business about the princeling. Now, was that anything to drop on a poor dear Human male?"

McCoy watched Kirk smile the smile that charmed birds out of the trees, but the Commander remained stony. Finally Kirk sobered again. "I do apologize, Commander. Most seriously and in dead earnest. Will you forgive me?"

Finally she nodded. "Let us not use metaphors like 'dead earnest.' We have had quite enough of death."

"Yes," Kirk said. "Friends?"

She nodded and offered him the Romulan gesture of crossed wrists. "And allies. But should you ever do anything of the sort again, I will make you wish that you only had to worry about being a princeling—poor dear."

Finally Kirk laughed, but it was a little shaky. "Understood," he said—and swayed a little.

James went Romulan pale and was suddenly at Jim's elbow, moving him to a bed, the Vulcan joining him on the other elbow, and McCoy was across the distance practically in a standing jump with his scanner. But as far as he could tell it was just cumulative shock—God, Jim was entitled, and he wouldn't rest—and a couple of new crunches from the fight. That—and it took a lot out of him to kill. Let alone to kill Omne.

"Get out of here and let me get to my patient," McCoy said flatly, and looked at the Vulcan. "Patients. Later for the galaxy."

James nodded. "Exactly," he said in the command tone. "Bones, take over. Sit on 'em if you have to. Jim, Spock, in bed. Long rest. That's an order." He moved to the intercom. "Scotty?"

"Aye, Captain!"

James raised a Romulan eyebrow which said: close enough. "Thanks, Scotty. Beautiful job."

"Mr. Spock's idea. He said you wanted a way to shoot a gun out of a man's hand. Just a wee tuning up of the antibiological circuit we use to rid cargo of rats and other vermin. Sort of the opposite problem."

"Not so opposite," James said thoughtfully. "It got rid of a—wolf."

Did it? McCoy thought, working over Kirk.

"Aye, sir," Scott said, a little doubtfully.

"Mr. Scott, prepare to head out, warp factor seven. Lay in a course to resume our interrupted mission. Prepare for intra-ship beaming. The Commander will give you the coordinates. Take the con until further notice. Kirk out." There was just the faintest hesitation on the name.

"Aye, sir."

James turned to the couches and came to stand beside the Commander. He took her hand—it looked for a moment rather more like she took his. He looked down at Kirk and across at Spock, who had made it as far as sitting on a couch.

"It won't get any easier," James said, glancing at the door. "And it can't get much harder. But—it won't be good-bye."

It finally came home to McCoy that they were really going to go—that he was: James. But dear God, it was still James T. Kirk.

How could they let him go?

And then it came back to McCoy in what way he and the Vulcan had had to be prepared to let James T. Kirk go, only a few hours ago.

Dear God, *that* had been the nightmare.

He looked at Spock and caught the same thought in the Vulcan's eyes. For a moment they shared a silent exchange which spoke of what they two alone had been through and shared, and of such comfort as McCoy could offer against the loss they would have to share now. But this loss they could bear. It would not be good-bye.

McCoy tried to send that certainty to the Vulcan.

"Thank you, Leonard," the Vulcan said without apology or explanation. He turned to James. "Gates of Hell, James."

McCoy completed the quotation in his mind. Yes.

James stood solemnly. Then his mouth flickered in the smile which had not changed. "We've broken out of worse places, Spock. Today."

"The valley of the shadow of death. . ." Spock said, looking at James as if he were a triumph. "That is what we broke out of today—if it takes years to recapture the victory and make it final."

Spock looked at Jim Kirk, too, and Kirk nodded. "We have years. And we have—James. New friends—" He looked at the Commander. "If you don't get him out of here this minute, I'm going to start to worry about the princeling again."

"*I'll* worry about the princeling," James said.

The Commander shook her head. "*I* will."

McCoy sighed. "So say we all," he said.

And he saw that he had done it again as the Commander and James made it out the door.

Space: the Final Frontier. ™
These are the voyages of the Starship Enterprise ™ ...

STAR TREK®:
THE CLASSIC EPISODES

adapted by James Blish
with J.A. Lawrence

Here are James Blish's classic adaptations of *Star Trek*'s dazzling scripts in three illustrated volumes. Each book also includes a new introduction written especially for this publication by D.C. Fontana, one of *Star Trek*'s creators; David Gerrold, author of "The Trouble With Tribbles;" and Norman Spinrad, author of "The Doomsday Machine."

Explore the final frontier with science fiction's most well known and beloved captain, crew and starship, in these exciting stories of high adventure—including such favorites as "Space Seed," "Shore Leave," "The Naked Time," and "The City on the Edge of Forever."

6 DECADES FREE

By subscribing to **Analog Science Fiction & Fact** you'll receive a **FREE** copy of **6 Decades—The Best of Analog** with your paid subscription. Analog readers have enjoyed over 60 years of penetrating, absorbing science fiction and science fact. From the earliest and continuing visions of cybernetics to our ultimate growth in space—Analog is the forum of the future. Let the pages of Analog expand the realm of your imagination...as today's fiction turns to tomorrow's fact.